Death
Waxed Over

Tim Myers

BERKLEY PRIME CRIME, NEW YORK

THE BERKLEY PUBLISHING GROUP
Published by the Penguin Group
Penguin Group (USA) Inc.
375 Hudson Street, New York, New York 10014, USA
Penguin Group (Canada), 90 Eglinton Avenue East, Suite 700, Toronto, Ontario M4P 2Y3, Canada
(a division of Pearson Penguin Canada Inc.)
Penguin Books Ltd., 80 Strand, London WC2R 0RL, England
Penguin Group Ireland, 25 St. Stephen's Green, Dublin 2, Ireland (a division of Penguin Books Ltd.)
Penguin Group (Australia), 250 Camberwell Road, Camberwell, Victoria 3124, Australia
(a division of Pearson Australia Group Pty. Ltd.)
Penguin Books India Pvt. Ltd., 11 Community Centre, Panchsheel Park, New Delhi—110 017, India
Penguin Group (NZ), Cnr. Airborne and Rosedale Roads, Albany, Auckland 1310, New Zealand
(a division of Pearson New Zealand Ltd.)
Penguin Books (South Africa) (Pty.) Ltd., 24 Sturdee Avenue, Rosebank, Johannesburg 2196, South Africa

Penguin Books Ltd., Registered Offices: 80 Strand, London WC2R 0RL, England

This is a work of fiction. Names, characters, places, and incidents either are the product of the author's imagination or are used fictitiously, and any resemblance to actual persons, living or dead, business establishments, events, or locales is entirely coincidental. The publisher does not have any control over and does not assume any responsibility for author or third-party websites or their content.

DEATH WAXED OVER

A Berkley Prime Crime Book / published by arrangement with the author

PRINTING HISTORY
Berkley Prime Crime mass-market edition / October 2005

Copyright © 2005 by Tim Myers.
Cover art by Mary Ann Lasher.
Cover design by George Long.
Interior text design by Kristin del Rosario.

ISBN: 0-425-20637-8

BERKLEY® PRIME CRIME
Berkley Prime Crime Books are published by The Berkley Publishing Group,
a division of Penguin Group (USA) Inc.,
375 Hudson Street, New York, New York 10014.
The name BERKLEY PRIME CRIME and the BERKLEY PRIME CRIME design are trademarks belonging to Penguin Group (USA) Inc.

PRINTED IN THE UNITED STATES OF AMERICA

10 9 8 7 6 5 4 3 2 1

3 1223 07224 5773

To Patty and Emily,
The true candles lighting my way.

Absence diminishes small loves and increases great ones,
as the wind blows out the candle and fans the bonfire.

—François La Rochefoucauld

One

I didn't hear the shot that killed Gretel Barnett, even though her life was extinguished just fifteen feet from where I stood. There were too many other explosions filling the air, happy merriments celebrating New Conover Founder's Day. It would have been tragic enough if she'd been a random face in the crowd, but there was something that made it infinitely worse. Gretel was my chief competitor, selling candles and supplies two miles from my own candleshop in Micah's Ridge, North Carolina. From the way things appeared, I was going to be running short of wick myself if I didn't come up with who had snuffed out her flame.

TWO WEEKS EARLIER, I'd finally worked up the nerve to tell my lone employee, Eve Pleasants, that At Wick's End was going to have a vendor's table at the New Conover celebration. I delayed sharing the news as long as I could, knowing that she would most likely take it with less than gracious acceptance. I owned the candleshop, along with the rest of River's Edge—a former warehouse and factory now converted into a complex of shops, offices and my apartment—perched on the edge of the Gunpowder River. But I was less than the master of my own domain, though I cherished At Wick's End, with its aisles full of waxes, wicks and molds; racks of tools and pots; shelves of powders; tubs of gel and sheets of honeycombed wax. Most of all, I loved the candles. Whether squatty and fat or long and tapered, shaped like stars or bowls, poured into teapots or watering cans, I found beauty in them all. My great-aunt Belle had left me the property, along with a hefty mortgage and the legal stipulation that I couldn't sell the complex until I'd run the candleshop for five years. I never could have imagined that I'd so quickly grow to love the place.

My great-aunt had also left me Eve, an older, dour, heavyset woman with a knack for candlemaking and a disposition that forced me to tiptoe around my own business most of the time. She was my erstwhile assistant and would-be candlemaking conscience, and little by little, we were finding a way to work together.

We weren't there yet, though. She took the news about like I'd expected. "Harrison Black, I've told you before that we never bothered with that fair. Belle and I didn't believe the return on our investment would be worth the trouble and the expense."

"We're not doing it for the profit," I said. "At least not strictly for that," I added, knowing that the bottom line was crucial to keeping my shop afloat.

"Then why put ourselves through it?" she asked.

"With the new candleshop opening in town, we need to make our presence felt. Let's face it, we're probably going to lose some customers, and they have to be replaced." Flickering Lights—our new competition in the form of a candle franchise that covered the world—was about to open a store in Micah's Ridge. Located in the revitalized downtown business district, it was declaring itself an upscale version of At Wick's End all over town. The owner was named Gretel Barnett, a no-nonsense older woman with stylish silver hair and a trim waistline. She had introduced herself a month before opening her shop, coming into At Wick's End, studying the place with a sharp eye, then declaring her intention to open a candle franchise of her own. At least no one could say she had skulked into town. I didn't like being portrayed as the thrift version of candleshops in the area, but so far I hadn't been able to do anything about it. The Founder's Day Celebration was my chance to make a statement of my own, and I wasn't about to let it slip by.

"Do you honestly think it will help our sales here enough to matter?" Eve asked.

"It will increase our profile locally, since New Conover's not that far away, and I'd say that's pretty important. You told me when I first came to At Wick's End that you and Belle used to do these street fairs all the time."

"It was always more your great-aunt's desire than mine."

It was pretty obvious the direction our conversation was taking, and there was no way I was going to endure an entire day at the fair listening to her litany of complaints. Inspiration suddenly struck. "Eve, you don't have to go. You can keep the store open while I'm there."

"You can't run a booth by yourself, Harrison."

There was no way I was giving in that easily. "I'll get Heather to watch it for me if I need to step away for a minute or two. We're setting up side by side." Heather Bane ran The New Age, her self-described serenity shop filled with things like crystals and personal pyramids. Heather's place was right next door to my candleshop at River's Edge, and she was participating in the fair as well.

Eve huffed once, then said, "I don't suppose there's any way to talk you out of this, is there? Very well, if you insist, I'll help you do it correctly."

"You know, I think this way is actually better," I said. "We might even make a profit if you stay here and keep the shop open." If Eve was waiting for me to tell her I couldn't do it without her, she was going to be disappointed. Over the past few months I'd gotten pretty good with the basics of candlemaking, and there weren't many questions at the shop I couldn't answer on my own, not that I was ready to run the place without her. Eve taught several of our classes at night, and I was the first to admit she handled group sessions better than I did. Still, my income for the store through teaching exceeded hers, and would continue to do so as long as I had my star student, Mrs. Jorgenson, a rich dilettante who had suddenly taken a passionate fancy to candlemaking. Together, we'd explored one-on-one basic candlemaking techniques for rolled candles and dipped ones as well. We'd touched briefly on pouring candles, but Mrs. Jorgenson had recently told me she'd like to get back to that technique before we got into gel candles, and with what she was paying me for private lessons, she could certainly dictate our schedule if she wanted to. It was almost a crime to charge her so much for something I enjoyed doing, but I had to constantly remind myself that I was in business to make money.

From her expression, it was pretty obvious that Eve was

wavering, so I decided to end our discussion. "Then it's settled. You keep At Wick's End open for our regular customers during the fair, and I'll see what I can do about getting some new ones."

Before Eve could protest any more, the bell over the front door jingled and Pearly Gray, retired psychologist and current handyman to all of River's Edge, said, "Harrison, I need a moment of your time if you can spare it."

A smooth escape was exactly what I needed. As I walked over to him, I asked, "What can I do for you, Pearly?"

He frowned, then said, "I hate to do this to you right now, but I need a break from my duties."

Pearly hadn't taken a day off since I'd inherited the River's Edge complex, and I had no idea what arrangements for vacation he'd made with Belle. "How much time do you need? We could probably spare you for a week or two if we had to."

He looked startled by the offer. "Goodness no, it's nothing like that. I just need tomorrow off. I have to help a friend." He said the last with his gaze downcast, and I wondered what kind of help he'd be supplying, but it was none of my business.

"That would be fine," I said.

"Thank you, Harrison." Pearly grabbed my hand in both of his and shook it vigorously. After he was gone, I realized that he was much more enthusiastic with his thanks than he'd needed to be. What was Pearly up to?

No matter. I really didn't have time to delve into my handyman's private life. I had a table display to prepare for the event, just one more task I'd never attempted before in my life. There was one thing I could say about running At Wick's End: just when I thought I had a handle on things, something new popped up to show me just how wrong I was.

I'd finally gotten Eve to accept the idea of the Founder's Day table by asking her opinions on my display plans, and I thought I had her won over when a frown shadowed her face.

"What is it now?" I asked. "Have you thought of another objection to the idea?"

"It's not that. Look who's coming in."

I turned to see Becka Lane, my onetime girlfriend, rush inside At Wick's End. Her lustrous blonde hair—usually perfect in appearance—was tousled, and one edge of her blouse was coming out of her short skirt's waistband. My sarcastic comment died in my throat when I saw her face, though. There was a look of pure, raw fear in her eyes that startled me with its intensity.

"Becka, what is it? What's wrong?"

She rushed toward me, then glanced back at the door. "That man . . . he's back. He's after me. Harrison, you'll protect me, won't you?"

"Protect you from what?" I looked out the bay window in front of the shop, but I couldn't see anyone nearby. "Becka, there's nobody out there. What are you talking about?"

She nearly screamed. "Go look for yourself. I'm telling you, he's out there."

I picked up a large wrought-iron candle stand by the door and walked out of the shop, scanning the parking lot and walkway in front of the complex. Aside from an elderly couple looking in the windows of the new antique shop and a group of young women going into The Pot Shot pottery, there was no one around.

At I came back inside, Becka grabbed my shoulder. "Did you see him? Did you?"

"Nobody's out there," I said.

"Harrison, he must have ducked into one of the shops. I've never seen his face; he always hides in the shadows. I'm telling you, he was there a minute ago."

I led her to the office in back, offered her my chair, then took Eve's regular seat. "You need to take a deep breath and tell me what's been happening." Becka wasn't my favorite ex-girlfriend, not after I'd learned about her argument with my late great-aunt Belle just before she'd died, but we'd meant something to each other once, and I couldn't turn my back on that. It would have probably been easier to help a stranger, someone I had no history with, but regardless of what had gone on before between us, I couldn't abandon her now.

"It started last week," she said softly. "At first I thought it was just my imagination, but I kept getting this creepy feeling that I was being watched, you know? He's not going to be content just shadowing me, I realize that now. He's trying to engage me in something, but I don't know what to do about it."

"Are you saying he's done something more direct?" I asked.

"Harrison, I'm not imagining this. I wouldn't. He's stalking me, I know it."

"Take it easy, I believe you."

After she hesitated a second, she added, "It's getting worse." I could see her shiver slightly as she continued. "Today when I got back to my car from grocery shopping, there was a note on my windshield that said, I NEED TO SEE MORE OF YOU, printed out in big block letters."

"What did you do?"

"I panicked," she said. "Normally I'm not afraid of anything or anybody, but this is really creeping me out. I tore the note up and drove straight here. He must have followed me."

"You came to me?" I couldn't believe Becka was willing to admit she needed me for anything.

"Harrison, we may have had our problems in the past, but you're the one person in the world I know I can always count on."

Becka prided herself on her independence, so I knew what that statement must have cost her. "The first thing we need to do is call the sheriff."

"Do you honestly think he'll be able to help me?"

"Truthfully, I'm not sure what he can do at this point, but we still need to let him know what's going on."

She snapped, "What's it going to take, an all-out attack from the man? I can't stand feeling this way, but I won't let the police think I'm a fool, either. Forget it."

I stood and leaned against the wall. "I just don't know what else I can do. I'm here if you need me, you know that."

She stood and put a hand on my shoulder. "Believe me, I know that, Harrison. Honestly, I feel better just telling you about it."

"Are you sure you don't want to phone the police? I'd be glad to make the call for you."

She shook her head. "No, not until I've got something to show them. It was foolish of me to tear up that note, I realize that now." She hesitated a moment, then added, "Do you know what I'm going to do? The next time I see him, I'm going to turn around and confront him."

It was a lousy idea, but I couldn't say it that openly. "Do you honestly think that's the best course of action to take?"

"Don't worry about me, Harrison, I'll be fine. I'm betting once he knows I'm not afraid of him anymore, he'll run away like a scared little boy." She opened her purse and pulled out a red cylinder. "Besides, I've got this Mace for protection if he tries anything."

"At least let me walk you to your car."

She nodded. "I'd appreciate that."

Eve was trying her best not to let on that she'd been eavesdropping when Becka and I walked toward the front door. "I'll just be a minute," I told her.

"Take your time," Eve said, though her gaze never left my ex-girlfriend.

I walked Becka to her car, all the while searching the parking lot and shops for her stalker. No one matching her vague description was in sight, but that didn't mean he wasn't lurking somewhere nearby. Becka unlocked her car and got in, but not before she searched the backseat. She started the engine, locked the doors, then rolled down her window. "Thanks, Harrison."

"I didn't do anything," I said with a grin.

"You were here for me when I needed you," she said simply.

Before she drove off, I said, "Be careful. Becka, I'm not happy about leaving it like this. You really should let the police know what's going on."

"If he does anything else, I will. I promise."

I had an uneasy feeling as I watched Becka drive off. If anything happened to her now, I'd feel partially responsible. I decided to call the sheriff when I got back inside despite her objections.

Eve asked, "What was that all about?"

"Becka believes somebody's after her. Why don't you listen while I call the sheriff? It'll be easier to get the details that way." I got Sheriff Morton on the telephone and told him everything Becka had told me. Eve's eyes grew wide at the description of the stalking, but it had little effect on the sheriff. A man named Coburn had been the sheriff when I'd first inherited River's Edge, but he'd been voted out of office just after I'd discovered who had murdered Belle. Morton was a little better, but not by much.

When I was finished, he said, "It could be stalking, or it could be that your girlfriend's got an overactive imagination."

"She's not my girlfriend," I said automatically. "I admit that Becka's had a flair for the dramatic in the past, but I'd still feel better if you talked to her. You didn't see her face when she came into the shop."

Morton hesitated, then said, "Give me her name and address." After I did, he said, "Tell you what, I'll have a black-and-white unit check on her later. That's the best I can do."

"I'll take it. Thanks, Sheriff."

"No problem."

After I hung up, Eve said, "Well, she certainly had every reason to be upset, didn't she?"

"I can't imagine her coming to me for protection," I said. While I was an inch shy of six feet tall, I was a good fifteen pounds overweight. Besides, I hadn't been in a real fight since the fifth grade. I couldn't imagine being anyone's guardian.

"Come now, Harrison, it's obvious the woman has faith in your ability to protect her."

"I don't know why she'd think that."

"Perhaps you're all she has," Eve said simply.

"If that's true, then she's got more problems than someone stalking her." I was worried about Becka, but there was nothing I could do about her situation. She'd call if she needed me—there was no doubt in my mind about that—so I tried to put her out of my mind and get back to the business of running my candleshop. Still, I was uneasy every time I heard the telephone ring, wondering if it might be her, in some kind of trouble I might not be able to fix.

Two

THE anointed day for the festival came soon enough. I'd spoken with Becka a few times since the sheriff had checked on her, but she'd had no more encounters with the stranger since that day at River's Edge. Maybe he'd followed her home and had seen her talking to the policc, or maybe seeing me armed with a candle stand had been enough to scare him off. Whatever the reason, Becka appeared to be safe.

The late-fall weather for the Founder's Day Celebration in New Conover was perfect as an unseasonably warm breeze brushed away the touches of winter's impending cold. Far too late in the season to be called Indian summer, the warmth was no less welcome, especially to those of us who were slated to be out in it all day. Our part of North Carolina could have six inches of snow one week, then temperatures could soar into the seventies the next, and by sheer luck, the event organizers had scheduled the celebration during a day more fit for spring than winter.

Even at 7 A.M., I found myself sweating as I unloaded my truck in the early dawn. I'd come to think of the Ford that way, though I'd inherited it, along with nearly all the rest of my worldly goods, from Belle. I just wished she could be there with me right now, the two of us working side by side.

I was setting up near the old County Courthouse, now operated as a museum dedicated to the area's past. The two-hundred-year-old granite building was draped in bunting and decorated with dozens of flags for the festivities. New Conover was the county seat, located twenty minutes from Micah's Ridge.

"Hey, are you going to daydream all morning, or are you going to help me with my stuff?" I was glad that Heather Bane and I had decided to set up together. I didn't feel quite so vulnerable with a friendly face nearby. Heather's long blonde hair was pulled back in its standard ponytail, and she wore a tie-dyed T-shirt with her jeans.

I slid her table off the truck bed and said, "I was just thinking about Belle."

"She would have loved this, Harrison," Heather said as we set her table on its folding legs.

"Eve wasn't sure my presence here would be worth the effort and cost," I said. "I'm starting to wonder if she was right. Are you worried about making anything more than what you paid for the display fee?"

Heather laughed. "Don't get cold feet now. We'll both do fine. I've got Mrs. Quimby and Esmeralda watching the store and Eve's keeping your candleshop open, so we'll make out all right." Mrs. Quimby was Heather's lone part-time employee, while Esmeralda was her cat and erstwhile queen of The New Age.

I finished transferring the boxes in the truck bed to our

tables, then said, "Watch our stuff, would you? I've got to go park in the vendor lot."

I had to walk three blocks back to our tables after I moved the truck, but it was a glorious morning, and I didn't mind the stroll. I love early morning; it's my favorite time of day, before the whole world's awake and bustling around. As I passed table after table, I watched the crews set up, most of them obviously seasoned in preparing their displays. I still didn't know exactly how I was going to arrange my space, but there would be time, since the festivities didn't officially open until 9 A.M. I was nearly back to my booth when I ran into Gretel Barnett, the femme candlemaker herself.

"Hi, Gretel. I didn't know you were going to be here," I said, trying to hide my displeasure at her presence.

In a voice that rang out over the nearby sounds of folks setting up, she proclaimed, "It's a free country, Harrison. I could hardly stand by and watch you steal all my customers from me, now could I?"

"How in the world can you accuse me of stealing anything? You're the one encroaching on my territory." My voice tends to get louder when I'm excited or angry, and I noticed that a few nearby vendors were watching us intently. So be it. I wasn't sure what had brought out this new belligerent attitude of hers, but I wasn't going to let her get away with it.

She retorted, "This is the land of democracy, the American way. Surely you're not against America." Gretel nearly shouted her last words, and we were getting more and more attention.

Fighting to keep my voice calmer than I felt, I said, "I won't give you the satisfaction of making me lose my temper in public. This didn't have to be personal, but you're making it that way."

"I'm going to bury you," she said, not softening her voice at all. "You and your sad little candle store."

As she stalked off, I felt my face redden. I was still steaming as I approached my table.

Heather asked, "What was that all about?"

"You heard?"

"Everyone here heard you two. Did she just accuse you of being un-American?"

"I thought we were going to have a friendly little competition between candleshops, but I guess I was wrong. Now it's personal."

"Harrison, you need to try to get along with her."

A lecture was the last thing I needed at the moment. "Heather, I don't need you as my conscience. I wasn't the one who started this."

We didn't share more than half a dozen words after that, each left to our own thoughts. What in the world had brought out that kind of attack from Gretel? She'd been abrupt when she'd come into my shop before, but she hadn't been insulting.

As I worked on my display, I couldn't help wondering what had set her off. She'd been open only a week, but I was already seeing a sharp drop in my sales. It hadn't really surprised me. Gretel had the wisdom of her franchise to back her up and help her keep from making some of the mistakes that had nearly ruined me.

I'd been wondering if she was going to wipe out my business, and then she actually had the nerve to make her declaration to the world that she was going to bury me! If I lost it all, it wasn't going to be without a fight. I was determined to prove her wrong, no matter what it took. If that meant extending my hours and deepening my discounts, I could get by on less if I had to. At least I had all of River's Edge to help defray my expenses, while she had only her stand-alone shop. I just wish I knew what kind of cash reserves she had. Buying the franchise couldn't have been cheap, and I knew their support only went so far.

Starting Monday morning, I was going to plan an assault on Flickering Lights that would drive one of us out of business; I just hoped it wasn't At Wick's End. I loved my candleshop too much to just let it sink quietly into oblivion.

But if a fight was what Gretel Barnett wanted, then she was going to get one.

I LAID OUT my display, including a free giveaway drawing for one of Eve's most ornately carved candles. It was a work of art, though she hadn't liked it when I'd said that, and I was hoping we could get enough names and addresses with the entry forms to start a newsletter for At Wick's End. It was an idea I'd picked up from my research on making small businesses grow, and I was willing to try just about anything. Another article had said that if you could get the kids interested in your crafts, a lot of times the parents followed, so I also laid out some sheets of lavender beeswax that had been damaged in our storeroom. They weren't good enough to sell, since one edge of the delicate sheets had been crushed in storage, but I'd trimmed the bad parts away with a pizza crust cutter, and they'd be perfect for kids to play with.

Heather watched my progress, then said, "If you need more space, I can give you a corner of my table."

"Is it too much?"

"No, I'm starting to wish I'd done more myself. It looks like you've done your homework on self-promoting."

"Let's just see if it works."

I finished displaying the candles and inexpensive kits I'd brought along to sell, and finally I was ready. Ten feet away, I noticed Gretel was watching me from her table, but I wasn't about to say a word or acknowledge her presence again if I could help it. My signs were all homemade—and they looked it—but hers sported a professional appearance that was just too sleek to be her own work. There were carefully crafted displays that showed some of the simplest steps to making candles, and even I had to admit they were very well done. It wasn't a fair fight since she had a franchise's expertise to draw from, but that didn't really matter to me anymore. I was ready for her. She'd thrown the gauntlet down, and if she was having second thoughts about taking me on, she was going to have to make the first move at brokering some kind of peace between us.

Gretel appeared to start my way once or twice before changing her mind and backtracking to her spot. She was either going to start Round Two of our fight, or she was coming over to apologize, but as the gates opened and people started coming in, she frowned and settled into her seat. Though she was new to the area, somehow Gretel had finessed a prime spot for her display, and I wondered if she'd paid off the organizers. Her table was five feet away from the Civil War cannon that adorned the grounds, a great attraction for the visitors coming in. I'd heard that the Founder's Day committee had wanted to drape the cannon in bunting too, but the Sons of the South had put their collective feet down. That cannon was a relic from history, they'd argued, a captured trophy from a Yankee ship, won with the spilled blood of their ancestors, not some prop for the show. I was near the granite steps, and I could see the old courthouse bell on the other side of the lawn from where I stood. It had been at the county seat since the mid-1800s, serving the early citizens of New Conover, and then retired and covered by a stone hutch. The cannon and bell were the two best-known artifacts in the entire town.

The flow of visitors picked up considerably, and I didn't have time to worry about Gretel Barnett anymore. Before long I had a great many lookers, a handful of buyers, and a good start on my mailing list. I was also starving, since I'd forgotten all about breakfast in my haste to get set up in time.

During a lull, I said, "Heather, are you hungry?"

"No, I always eat a big breakfast before I do these fairs. There's barely time to turn around during the day."

"That was smart of you," I said.

She studied me a second, then said, "Harrison, I'll watch your table if you want to go grab a quick bite."

"I hate to ask you to do that," I said, determined to suffer through my mistake.

"Hey, we're covering for each other here, remember? You go now and you can watch my table when I grab lunch for us later. It will be really busy then."

"Busier than now?"

She scanned the crowds. "Just wait. On a day like today, folks are itching for a reason to get outside. We're going to make some money, my friend, just wait and see."

A burst of firecrackers suddenly went off twenty feet from us, and I could see more streamers dancing in the air. The noise had started the moment Founder's Day opened, and if the pyrotechnics kept up, I was in for a major headache before it was time to wrap up and go home.

"I'd better go now then," I said. "Do you want anything? How about some aspirin?"

"No, I'm fine. To be honest with you, I kind of like the noise. It makes me feel alive."

I cut through the back way toward the concession area rather than fight the crowd. It was roped off for the vendors only, and I was glad to have the shortcut. Gretel didn't even notice as I passed within three feet of her table. She was busy selling an expensive candlemaking kit to a woman with frosted hair piled high on her head in a beehive. We sold the same kits ourselves at our shop, but not for as much as she was charging. I kicked myself for not bringing more of the high-dollar items too, but I'd only had so much room on my table with my giveaway and kids area. As I walked to the concession area, I nearly tripped over a clown perched on the courthouse steps. Dressed in full makeup and costume, he looked more at home at the celebration than I did. Maybe Eve had been right. I probably should have stayed home.

I grabbed a sausage-and-egg biscuit and an orange juice from one of the food vendors and nearly knocked Pearly down as I turned around to head back to my table.

"I didn't know you were coming to the festivities," I said.

Pearly said, "A man has to do something with his time off. Harrison, there's something I need to discuss with you."

"Walk with me back to my table and we can talk along the way," I said. I didn't want to leave Heather alone for too long.

He glanced toward my spot, then shook his head. "I'd rather not, if you don't mind. We could go over to the courthouse steps away from the crowd, though."

"Pearly, I'd love to be able to do that, but Heather's watching my table for me, and I can't leave her alone. Is it something that can wait?"

"I suppose so," he said reluctantly.

"Good. We'll talk about it first thing Monday morning then."

I started back toward my table, wolfing down the biscuit as I walked. I'd probably get indigestion from the fast meal on my feet, but I didn't have much choice. I tossed the wrapper and empty carton of juice into a trash can near the cannon, wiped my hands on my bandana, then ran my hand around the inside rim of the pitted metal of the empty barrel for good luck before I walked back to my vending spot amid the noise of firecrackers exploding all around me.

While I was still fifteen feet away from my table, I noticed a commotion out of the corner of my eye and turned just in time to see Gretel crumple to the ground, knocking her display down in the process.

At first I thought she'd had a heart attack, but as I raced closer, I saw a blood stain blossom on the back of her dress.

During one of the constant fireworks bursts, someone had taken the opportunity to kill my chief competition.

Before I could take it all in, a woman in her mid-forties pointed right at me and screamed, "He shot her. That's the man who shot her."

Three

"I didn't shoot her," I protested, feeling my legs weaken with the accusation.

The woman was not to be deterred, though. She screamed hysterically, "He threw the gun into that trash can! I saw him do it!"

Sheriff Morton, the law enforcement chief for the entire county, was beside me in a heartbeat. His ruddy complexion and brown hair were in sharp contrast to his predecessor's washed-out appearance, but I couldn't count either of the men as friends. "Harrison, what's she talking about?"

"She's nuts, Sheriff, I didn't do it."

He looked toward Gretel's motionless form and commanded, "Wait right here. I'll straighten this out." While Morton went to check on Gretel, my accuser stood there just staring at me, a few steps in front of the other onlookers.

I started toward the sheriff to see if there was anything I could do to help when the woman yelled, "He's trying to get away. Somebody stop him!"

"I'm not going anywhere," I said heatedly. "I'm just going to check on Gretel."

Morton growled over his shoulder at me, "Get back where you were. Now."

I retreated back to my spot, feeling a hundred pairs of eyes focused on me. The crowd had already marked me as the shooter based on one nearsighted woman's accusation.

Heather hurried up beside me. "Harrison, what happened? Did you see it?"

"I was just coming back when she fell over. I thought she was having a heart attack at first. Then I saw the blood. This lunatic," I paused, pointing at my accuser, "thinks I shot her."

"Nonsense. Surely the sheriff will see that." I looked at Gretel just as the EMS crew was loading her into the back of an ambulance. There was an oxygen mask over her face, and they were moving with extreme urgency. At least she was still alive; that was something.

Morton rejoined me, and Heather took a step back. Evidently not far enough, though.

The sheriff said, "Hadn't you better get back to your table?"

"I think I'm needed here," Heather said stubbornly.

"Don't worry. If we need you, we'll let you know," Morton said.

After Heather reluctantly left, Morton asked, "Now what's this nonsense about you shooting Gretel Barnett?"

"I don't have a clue. That woman over there is either blind or she's insane, if you ask me."

Morton shook his head. "Stay. I'll be right back."

He had a whispered conversation with my accuser, and I saw her pointing at me again and again. Finally Morton started back in my direction. He brushed past me though and upended the trash can behind where I stood.

"What are you looking for?" I asked him.

"She claims she saw you shoot the victim, then throw the gun in here." As he rooted through the trash with a gloved hand, I said, "I threw away my orange juice container, not a gun. She's delusional."

Morton, in a softer voice, said, "Well, she also happens to be Wanda Klein. She's married to Hank Klein."

"The newspaper editor?" I asked.

"He's more than that; he's the publisher and owner of *The Gunpowder Gazette,* Harrison."

"Let me guess. You're taking her word over mine," I said.

"I have to investigate any lead I get. It's my job."

He stood, then said in a loud voice, "There's nothing's here."

"I saw what I saw," the woman said loudly. "He shot that poor woman in the back."

"For the last time, I didn't do a thing to her," I snapped.

One of the vendors who'd gathered in the crowd said, "You argued with her not an hour ago. There's no use denying it, a lot of us heard you."

This was getting out of hand. I said, "We had a disagreement, that's all. I didn't shoot her."

There were more murmurs from the crowd, then Morton said, "Folks, let's break this up. If you've got anything solid to report, come on up. Otherwise, I suggest you go about your business. We still don't know what happened here."

"*I* know," Wanda Klein said huffily as she stormed off into the crowd. As soon as she was gone, the rest of the group broke up until it was just the sheriff and me.

"Are you going to arrest me?" I asked.

"Motive and opportunity aren't enough, Harrison."

"Motive? You honestly think I'd shoot somebody because they were selling more candles than I was? That's ridiculous."

"Don't forget, we have an eyewitness," Morton said.

"She's either lying or she's wrong. So arrest me, if you're so convinced I did it."

"Harrison, losing your temper's not going to do either one of us any good."

"I don't appreciate being accused like that," I said.

"Then you're probably going to love this." He motioned to one of his deputies, who held a fishing tackle box in one hand. As he removed a swab and some liquid from the box, I asked, "What's this all about?"

"Just hold still. It'll only take a second."

The deputy rubbed different parts of both of my hands, studied the swabs, then shook his head. "Nothing here."

That's when I got it. "So now you know I didn't fire a gun today."

"Not without gloves on, anyway." Morton scratched his jaw. "It's procedure. You're not planning any big trips anytime soon, are you?"

I couldn't believe he thought I could have killed her. "No, you know where I spend all my time. If you need me, I'll be at River's Edge."

I walked off before he could say anything else and returned to my table. Most of the items for sale were gone. "What happened, did someone rob me while I was away?"

Heather said, "Are you kidding? As soon as that woman accused you of shooting Gretel, people started buying your stuff like crazy. I had half a dozen people make offers on the giveaway candle."

"That's just great." I started gathering up what was left of my display and shoved it all in a box I had stored under my table.

Heather said, "You're not quitting, are you?"

"I don't feel like staying here, not after what happened. Don't worry, I'll come back and help you break down this evening."

"Harrison, if you run now, folks are going to think you really did shoot her."

"And if I stay, I'll do myself more harm than good. I'll be back later to get our stuff, Heather. I promise."

The last place on earth I wanted to be was at that table. I needed to get out of New Conover, and if I had my way, I'd never come back.

I THOUGHT ABOUT going by the hospital to check on Gretel's condition, but I didn't want anyone to think I was there to finish what I'd started. I'd have to rely on the grapevine at River's Edge to tell me what was happening. No worries there, though. Millie Nelson, the woman who ran The Crocked Pot, had more information contacts than the police and the newspaper combined.

Millie handed me a cup of coffee, strong and black, the second I walked in the door of her café. An apron covered most of her ample form, and a frown creased on her lips as she saw me. "Harrison, are you all right?"

"I'm guessing you've already heard about the shooting."

She nodded. "One of the sheriff's men was here getting coffee. We heard the call go out on the radio. It's terrible, isn't it?"

"I didn't shoot her, Millie," I said flatly.

"Now who in the world thinks you did?"

"Some woman claims to be an eyewitness. She seems pretty convinced she saw me do it. All because I was standing at the wrong place at the wrong time and happened to throw my orange juice container away, though I still can't see how she thought it was a gun."

"Okay, back up. You lost me there."

"I grabbed a quick bite on the run, and as I was walking back to my sales table, I saw Gretel Barnett fall over. There was blood spreading out on the back of her dress, but before I could do anything, a woman named Wanda Klein started screaming that I was a killer."

Millie shook her head. "Wanda is a lunatic, everybody knows that."

"Try telling the sheriff. Maybe he'll believe you. I surely didn't make any headway with him. So you know this woman?"

"Oh yes," Millie said. "We've butted heads more times than I can count over the years. She once threatened to sue me because my coffee was too hot. I warned her, but she gulped it anyway. Honestly, nobody takes responsibility for their actions anymore."

"So what happened?"

"Her husband convinced her to buy her coffee somewhere else and drop it. At least one member of that family has some sense."

"So you don't think I have anything to worry about from her?" I asked.

"I wouldn't say that, Harrison. Evidently that was the first time in twenty-four years of marriage that Hank Klein ever disagreed with her, and he's been regretting it ever since. I wouldn't be surprised if you're mentioned in the article about what happened in tomorrow's paper. Prepare yourself for it."

"Maybe I need a lawyer," I said. The only one I really knew was Gary Cragg, one of my tenants and a man I thoroughly disliked. Did that matter, though? Lawyers and surgeons don't have to be cordial. What they needed to be was competent, and I'd heard that Cragg was that.

Millie patted my arm. "I'm sure it won't come to that."

"Let's hope you're right."

I got back to At Wick's End a good six hours before I was due. Eve was dusting shelves as I walked in.

"Harrison Black, tell me you're not here checking up on me."

"I trust you, Eve. There was a bit of trouble at the Founder's Day fair."

"They forgot to assign you a space? That's unforgivable."

"I wish that's all it was, but it's a little more serious than that. Gretel Barnett was shot an hour ago."

Eve dropped her dust rag without realizing it. "Shot? You can't be serious."

"I'm afraid I am. It gets worse. Morton is inclined to believe that I had something to do with it."

"And why would he think that? That's complete and utter nonsense."

"Believe it or not," I said, "there's an eyewitness, so she claims, but I didn't do it."

Eve said, "Harrison, I told you that fair would bring trouble."

She'd told me no such thing, but I wasn't in the mood to argue. "Listen, if you don't need me here, I'm going out on the water for a little while."

"I know we're enjoying a warm spell, but isn't it still a little brisk for kayaking?"

"I'll let you know when I get back."

I retrieved my kayak from the storage area for River's Edge and carried it down to the water. A long set of concrete steps led down to the water, and it made a handy place to put my boat in. I'd grown to love tooling around the Gunpowder River in my bright yellow kayak, but I wasn't looking for recreation today. What I needed was time away from the world, and a lot of it. I didn't always wear my life jacket, though Erin Talbot had chided me about always putting it on before I hit the water. She ran a canoe and kayak rental business and was an enthusiast, tackling whitewater all over the South. I personally enjoyed the flat, calm water of the Gunpowder. I put the kayak in the water, then stepped carefully inside. The first time I'd tried doing it on my own after buying the kayak, I'd capsized and managed to get thoroughly soaked in two feet of water. I was still a little shaky getting in and out, but once I was seated inside and had the blades in my hands, I was in my element. I thought about going downriver toward Erin's place. It was quite a paddle—I had plenty of time and a beautiful day—but what I really wanted was to be alone. I set off upstream, slicing through the mild current like I was on rails, and decided to work off some steam.

After paddling over an hour, I was nearly ready to turn around and go back to River's Edge when I spotted a tributary feeding into the Gunpowder that looked interesting. Pointing the tip of my boat toward it, I entered the narrower waterway and started exploring. A road bridge covered the water a hundred feet in, and as I paddled under it, I could hear the tinny echo of my oars as they dipped into the water. On a whim, I slapped the surface with the flat part of my paddle and was rewarded with a muted echo, as if the concrete and steel cushioned the blow. The underside of the bridge looked like corrugated steel, and as cars passed by above me, I heard an odd thrubbing noise. A part of me wanted to stay, but I knew it was time to turn around. My shoulders were beginning to ache, but I promised myself that I'd come exploring again sometime soon.

By the time I got back to my apartment, the kayak safely locked up again, I'd managed to ease a lot of the tension I'd been feeling.

Then I saw the blinking light on my answering machine.

The message was from Sheriff Morton, short and simple.

"She's dead, Harrison. We need to talk."

I WAS WAITING for Morton in my apartment when there was a heavy knock on the door.

Instead of the sheriff, I found Markum on my doorstep.

"This isn't the best time for me to have company," I said.

The big man with unruly black hair ignored my comment and brushed past me. He'd shaved his wild beard, claiming it had gotten in his way on his last salvage and recovery mission. Though he was one of my tenants and fast becoming one of my best friends at River's Edge, I still had no real handle on what Markum really did for a living.

"I'm not here to hold your hand. What's this nonsense about you shooting some woman?"

"I didn't shoot anybody," I said wearily.

"I know that, you nitwit. What I want to know is why everybody thinks you did."

"A woman claims she saw me do it," I said, "And I'm having a tough time refuting it."

Markum put a meaty hand on my shoulder, and I felt the weight of it all the way down to my knees. "Harrison, give me her name and I'll have a talk with her before I go. I'm sure we can straighten this mess out."

"I wish it were that easy, but she's not budging. The bad thing is, she's married to the publisher of *The Gunpowder Gazette*."

"That just makes it a little more difficult, but still not impossible."

I didn't want to know what Markum had in mind. "Thanks, but let's see what happens with Morton first. He's due here any minute."

Markum shrugged. "Just let me know." He smiled softly, then added, "Good landlords are hard to come by, and I'd hate to have to look for another place. Listen, I've got something planned for this evening, something that's going to take me out of town for a few days, but if it would help, I'll postpone it, or cancel it altogether."

"Don't change your plans on my account. There's nothing you can do here."

Markum nodded. "If you're sure then, I'll go. I've got a honey of an opportunity, and I'm not sure it will wait."

There was another knock on the door. That had to be the sheriff. I started to say as much to Markum when he said, "I'll be on my way, but let me know if you change your mind."

"I will," I promised as I opened the door.

The sheriff was there, and the second he saw Markum, the frown on his face deepened, though I wouldn't have thought it was possible. He said curtly, "Markum."

"Sheriff," the big man answered, then walked out, but not before hesitating long enough to say to me, "Remember what I said."

I nodded, then shut the door behind him.

Morton said, "What was that all about?"

"He was offering to help me out with something," I said.

"Like what?"

"We've been talking about painting the hallway," I said, that being the first thing that popped into my head.

Morton snorted, but didn't push it. "You've got some real problems, my friend."

I felt my knees start to buckle. "You're going to arrest me? What's your evidence? I didn't shoot her."

"Take it easy. I'm not talking about me. I was just interviewed, if you want to call it that, by somebody from the newspaper. From the questions the reporter was asking, you're going to be the focus of their article tomorrow. I've got a feeling my 'no comments' are going to make things look bad for you. I thought you should know."

"Thanks, I appreciate that. I'm glad you believe me."

Morton shook his head. "I'm not saying I do, and I'm not saying I don't, but I'll be dipped in tar if I'm going to let them smear you without the facts. You might want to shut the candleshop for a few days."

"What, and let them win? I'm not going anywhere. I'm innocent, whether anyone believes me or not."

Morton said sadly, "And you're naïve enough to think that matters? Harrison, I've got a feeling you're about to get hammered."

"I can take it. I'm not going to hide," I said.

He looked around. "Isn't that what you're doing up here? Eve's getting overrun with customers downstairs. If you don't care about yourself, at least shut the place down for her sake."

"I didn't realize she needed help," I said, mustering as much dignity as I could. "I'll go help her."

"I wouldn't, if I were you."

"Well, you're not me, are you?"

"It's your funeral," the sheriff said as he followed me out of my apartment.

"You might want to work on your choice of expressions, Sheriff," I said as we walked down the steps together.

He shook his head, then held the door at the bottom of the landing for me. "You want some crowd control? I'm on my way over to Flickering Lights, but I can send one of my people over to help you out here."

"I'm sure we can handle it." I started to change my mind when I followed his gaze and saw that most of the parking lot was full. At Wick's End was being overrun with customers, something I'd been dreaming about since I'd taken over.

It was a wonderful lesson in being careful what you wish for.

Four

I'D never seen the candleshop so crowded, even though few of our visitors had any of our products or supplies in their hands. It appeared they'd all shown up to get a look at the accused killer. Well, if I was going to be on display, I was going to at least make some money from it.

I said loudly, "My name's Harrison Black. If you're here to buy candlemaking supplies, welcome. But if you're in At Wick's End for any other reason, I'm going to have to ask you to leave."

"Why aren't you under arrest?" a woman asked from the back of the store.

"Because I didn't kill Gretel Barnett." I suddenly had a thought. "If you have a question for me, I'll consider answering it as I'm ringing up your sale."

That caused a run on the shelves, and I saw Eve shaking her head in obvious disapproval. So be it. It was my candleshop, and my choice.

I walked to the register as the line started to form. A

woman handed me an expensive candlemaking kit, and as Eve rang it up, I said, "So what's your question?"

She said meekly, "I don't have one. I just wandered in to buy a kit. I hope that's all right."

"Of course it is," I said, feeling my face flush. "That's why we're here."

As she signed her credit card slip, the woman asked timidly, "So who was it you were supposed to have killed?"

"A fellow candlemaker, but it's not true."

She grabbed the bag from Eve and scurried out, hesitating to look back at me before she bolted through the door.

"Nicely done, Harrison," Eve said.

"So I wasn't right about everyone here. How much do you want to bet I'm right about most of the rest of them?"

She said, "I won't wager on a sure thing against me. You should hear some of the questions they've been asking me about you."

"No doubt I'm going to."

The next person in line said, "I saw the sheriff's patrol car out front. How'd you manage to convince him you didn't do it?"

Eve rang up his sale as I replied, "That one's easy. I'm not guilty."

"Hey, that's not much of an answer."

I shrugged and said, "Well, you didn't buy much, did you?"

That sent several people in line scurrying back to the shelves. I saw Eve watching me closely, and I asked, "Is that a smile?"

She chuckled softly. "Harrison, you're incorrigible, you know that, don't you?"

"So I've been told. How are we doing? I just about sold out my stock at the street fair."

Eve said, "Oh, we're having a banner day. I thought

about closing up as the crowd began to grow, but then I figured you'd want to stay open."

"I know you don't approve, but I appreciate it anyway."

She shook her head. "It's not up to me, but do you think Belle would have liked this?"

My great-aunt had loved candlemaking, so I'd been told by those closest to her, but she hadn't been that enthusiastic about marketing and promoting her wares. I was more concerned with the bottom line. Besides, it wasn't like I was trying to benefit from Gretel's murder. There was a good chance many of my regular customers might shun me until I was cleared of suspicion, and if I was going to keep my business afloat, I had to take advantage of the opportunities as they presented themselves.

"The thing you've got to remember is that Belle wanted the candleshop to stay open."

"But at what cost?"

I didn't know how to answer that, and fortunately the line was re-forming. There was a man up front with a basket full of our most expensive stock, both kits and actual candles that Eve and Belle had poured themselves. There was even one of my creations in his selection, something I felt very good about.

He handed the basket to Eve and said, "Take your time." He then turned to me and said, "Harrison, I understand there was bad blood from the start between you and Gretel Barnett."

"I wasn't exactly thrilled she was opening up a candleshop franchise so close to my shop, but I was willing to extend a neighborly hand to her."

"So what's this I hear about you two facing down in a shouting match this morning?"

This guy was relentless. "We had a disagreement, plain and simple. I'm sorry we won't have the opportunity to resolve it." And that was true. I felt a little sick that Gretel had died with bad blood brewing between us. She wasn't my favorite person in the world, but that still didn't mean I'd wanted to see her dead.

"Were you trying to bury her, like you said?"

I was doing my best not to lose my temper, but he was goading me. "She said she was going to bury me, not the other way around."

Finally Eve handed the man his card slip and he signed a hasty scrawl. As our customer took it, he said, "How about this relationship between the murder victim and one of the men here at River's Edge?"

Before I could answer, Eve said, "That's it, I knew your name sounded familiar. You're Tom Francis from *The Gunpowder Gazette,* aren't you?"

Oh, no! I hadn't realized I was being interviewed by the newspaper trying to hang me.

It was time to get rid of him. "Your shopping trip is over, and if you quote me, I'll deny every word of it."

He grinned and held up a tape recorder he'd retrieved from his front pocket. "Just try it."

As he scurried away, I said, "No more interviews. Buy or don't buy, I'm finished talking."

Half the people left at the announcement, but the rest lingered, hoping I'd change my mind. Eve said, "Nothing like locking the barn after the horses are all gone."

"Was it that bad? Did I say anything I shouldn't have?"

"Harrison, anything more than 'no comment' would have been too much."

I nodded. "Okay, maybe I should have given it a little more thought before I made my offer to them."

As Eve rang up another sale, she said, "I wouldn't waste my time worrying about it. Chances are they would have smeared you without the interview."

"If that's supposed to make me feel better, it's not working."

We got through the rest of the customers as closing time neared. I had had enough. "Why don't we lock up early? All I want to do is to go upstairs, take a hot shower and lose myself in a good book."

Eve said, "I thought our table was still at the fair? And weren't you supposed to help Heather take her display down, too?"

"Blast it, I forgot all about that."

"If you'd like, I suppose I could do it."

I shook my head. "No, I need to do it myself. I promised Heather I'd be there. You can shut down early if you'd like."

"You know how I feel about that. I'll stay open till the posted store hours are over."

"Just leave the deposit then. I'll make it this evening."

As I headed for the Ford truck, I was surprised to find a stranger waiting nearby for me. The alley behind River's Edge was as uninviting a place as I'd ever seen, not exactly a spot to linger. The man wore faded blue jeans and a jacket that had seen its share of rough weather. I thought about turning around and going back inside when he called my name.

"Harrison Black?"

"What can I do for you," I said, clinching my key ring in my fist.

"I want to talk to you about what happened today."

Yeah, well, I didn't. "Listen, I'm tired of answering questions. If you want to hear what really happened, read the newspaper tomorrow and believe just the opposite of what they'll be printing."

"No, you don't understand. I was at the fair today. I know you didn't kill her, because I saw who did."

"Are you serious? You need to go to the police."

He looked at River's Edge, then said, "This place must be worth a fortune."

"You'd have to ask the bank, it mostly belongs to them. What's that got to do with anything, anyway?"

"I was thinking maybe there'd be some kind of reward for coming forward," the man said softly.

"Get out of here,"

It was obviously not the kind of reaction he was expecting. "What do you mean? You're not going to pay me?"

"For telling the truth? I doubt you'd know it if it bit you on the leg. You probably weren't even at the fair today. Now go away."

He started to do as I'd asked, but paused before leaving the alley. "I could have seen it the other way just as easily, you know. If I give it enough thought, I might just remember that I saw you shoot her after all."

"You're bluffing now."

"What makes you think so?"

"Because there's nothing in it for you. Besides, I didn't do it."

I started the truck, my hands shaking from the confrontation. I couldn't believe anybody would try to shake me down for testifying to the truth. I realized that I'd better mention what had happened in the parking lot to the sheriff, just in case the lunatic tried to follow through with his threat of smearing me. I didn't need any more headaches at the moment than I already had. I finally managed to collect myself by the time I got to New Conover. It was just in time to break the displays down, too. Most likely I was in for another round of accusations before the night was over.

SURPRISINGLY, THINGS WERE quiet as Heather and I dismantled our tables. She said, "It's been like this all afternoon. The other vendors have been ignoring me, and the customers just stare as they walk by."

"I'm sorry," I said. "I feel responsible."

"It's not your fault, Harrison," she said. "I can't believe this happened right under our noses. Who would have had any reason to shoot Gretel Barnett?"

"Do you mean besides me?"

"Come on, I already told you, I know you didn't do it. But I can't help wondering who did."

"I don't have a clue. It could have been anybody. With all those firecrackers going off and the crowds milling around, it would be so easy for the killer to fade back into the mob. It's really none of my business."

Heather said, "You're joking, right? If anybody should be searching for the killer, it should be you."

"Why? Let the police handle it. Sheriff Morton's good at what he does."

"So you're willing to let your candleshop die, just like that? Harrison, there's something you don't understand. Just the implication that you had anything to do with Gretel's death could be enough to destroy your business. What she couldn't do in life, she might just manage in death."

"We had a load of customers today," I said in my own defense.

"Curiosity seekers," she said. "How many of your regular customers will come back if they think you're a killer? Do you think Mrs. Jorgenson is going to come waltzing in for more private lessons while you have this hanging over your head? Believe me, you'd better figure out who killed Gretel, and do it soon if you want to keep At Wick's End open."

I hadn't even thought about Mrs. Jorgenson. If I lost her business, which I very possibly could, my profit margin would sink like a stone in the Gunpowder. Heather was right. If I was going to keep my candleshop open, I was going to have to figure out who had killed the only other chandler in town.

AFTER UNLOADING HEATHER'S things back at River's Edge and putting the tables we'd used back into storage, I decided to pay a visit to Flickering Lights to see if I could find anything that might point to a reason Gretel had been murdered. Knowing Sheriff Morton, there was a good chance he would be there himself, and while he probably wouldn't be all that crazy about me just showing up, maybe I'd be able to find something out that would help clear me.

The new candleshop was lit up when I got there, though there was no sign that the police were anywhere around. Morton must have finished his search and moved on. I tried the door anyway and was surprised when it opened. As I walked inside the franchise store, I saw that Gretel didn't shy away from carrying the most expensive candle-making kits available, and the prices on her display pieces were nearly double mine. I didn't know if she'd be able to sell much of her wares, but with the mark-up she'd built in, it wouldn't take much for her to show a profit.

Two steps inside, I spotted an older gentleman behind the counter, nervously rubbing the bridge of his nose with one finger. He looked up and said, "I'm sorry, but we're not really open. I shouldn't even be here, but I don't know what else to do. The police just left."

He wasn't going to get rid of me that easily. "My name's Harrison Black. I wanted to come by and tell you I'm sorry for your loss."

He nodded. "I'm Jubal Grant. Of course I know you; you're the owner of At Wick's End. It's a delightful shop;

I've been there a time or two myself. Pearly speaks quite highly of you."

"You know Pearly?" What did my handyman have to do with any of this?

"Of course I do. I thought you knew. He and Gretel were quite an item; they had been for some time. In fact, he helped us set up here. I'm sorry; I shouldn't have said anything. I didn't realize it was a secret."

"No, that's fine. Pearly's free to do whatever he wants in his free time. I'm just surprised he didn't say anything to me about it before."

"He's the one who called and told me about Gretel. I understand you were there when it happened."

Great. "I don't know what he said, but—"

"Please, I've already heard the rumors, but I don't believe you had anything to do with Gretel's death, Mr. Black. Pearly agreed with me that it was a preposterous notion. She was feeling the pressure of your presence in Micah's Ridge, but I'm sure it wasn't personal. I can't imagine anyone seriously thinking you had anything to do with what happened to her today."

"Excuse my asking, but how well did you know her?"

He sighed. "Too well. I'm not just an errant employee, if that's what you're asking. Gretel was my second cousin. I suppose I'll have to deal with the funeral arrangements since her brother Hans isn't here, but I don't want to have to think about that now. I came back to the candleshop when the police called me. What a nightmare. The sheriff was most intrusive, asking all sorts of questions. I'm afraid I wasn't much help. Gretel and I had been drifting apart over the years. She called me last month to come help her with the candleshop, and I thought it would give us a chance to get reacquainted. I'm retired myself, but Micah's

Ridge sounded delightful, so I agreed to help out. I don't know what I'm going to do now."

"Do you have any idea who might have killed her?"

Jubal said, "Sheriff Morton asked me that same question. I haven't a clue who would want her dead. Gretel was so alive, do you know what I mean? And now her life's been snuffed out like an errant candlewick." He dabbed at a tear, then said, "She always said I was too dramatic. I'll miss so much about her."

"So what happens to the shop now?" I asked.

"I don't have a clue. I suspect all of her worldly goods were tied up in it. I suppose it will all go to her brother. She and Hans were estranged, but as twins, there was a real bond between them."

"Their parents named them Hans and Gretel?" The cruelty of some people when they named their children astounded me.

"I admit, it was a difficult time for them growing up. As if their being fraternal twins wasn't enough reason for them to stand out. Honestly, I don't even know how to find Hans. He dropped out of sight a dozen years ago, and no one in the family has seen him since. It's been thirty years since I've laid eyes on the man myself."

"There's no one else?"

He shook his head. "Our line is a dying branch of the family tree. Besides Hans, I'm all that's left."

I couldn't think of anything more to say, so I said, "If there's anything I can do, let me know, okay?"

Jubal shook my hand. "That's quite kind of you, Harrison. I may take you up on your generous offer later, after I've had a chance to find out where things stand. Thank you for stopping by."

I was at the door when Jubal said, "I just thought of

something. It's probably nothing, but we got the strangest telephone call yesterday. It upset Gretel quite a bit."

"Do you know who was calling?"

Jubal shook his head. "No, but I did hear something Gretel said. I'm not even sure I heard her correctly, I was standing six feet away. As I said, it's probably nothing."

"What did she say?" I asked.

He hesitated, then said, "I remember thinking how odd it was. I could have sworn she said, 'I'm not your wife,' but Gretel never married. I must have misunderstood her."

"Well, if you think of anything else, let me know."

Jubal said, "Am I correct in assuming you're looking into what happened to Gretel yourself?"

"I need to clear my name," I said simply.

"Of course, I understand. I'm willing to help you in whatever way I can, Harrison. Believe me, I know from experience that rumors can be fatal."

Five

WHEN I got back to my apartment at River's Edge, there were twenty-seven messages waiting for me on my machine. I couldn't face listening to them, though. I grabbed a jacket and headed up the secret hatch tucked away in my closet. As I climbed the rungs to the roof, I was glad no one else in the world had access to my hideaway. With twilight fading, the air was shifting from brisk to downright cold on the rooftop overlooking the Gunpowder River, but I was willing to put up with the plummeting temperatures to get away from the world for a while. I took out my lawn chair from the storage box and grabbed a heavy blanket. The wind had blown out the clouds, leaving a night sky filled with stunning starlight. We were far enough from Micah's Ridge to avoid most of the direct illumination, and when Pearly and I had installed lights around the complex, I'd made sure none of them interfered with my stargazing. Thinking of Pearly made me wonder what my handyman had been up to lately. The fact that he'd been dating and supporting my main competition was something I had a hard time getting used to. I'd thought Pearly was one of my staunchest allies at River's Edge, always there when I needed him, but I was beginning to wonder if I'd misplaced my trust in him. Had that been what he'd wanted to talk to me about at the fair? Was he having a guilty conscience about his relationship with Gretel? I wasn't sure how I was going to act toward him after the revelation that he'd been dating her. If I couldn't trust Pearly, then who could I trust? Who could I talk to about the churning issues stirring in my mind? As I sat there mulling over my dour thoughts, I began to think that solitude might not be the best thing for me at the moment. So where was there to turn to for a willing ear? I would have knocked on Markum's door, but he was away on one of his mysterious salvage and recovery trips. There was Millie, the woman who so ably ran The Crocked Pot. She was a good listener, but no doubt she was off somewhere enjoying time with her husband George. Heather had shown signs of roller-coaster reactions to things that had happened in the past, so I really didn't want to discuss the day's events with her, and Gary Cragg was a man I doubted I'd ever be able to trust. Sanora, our resident potter, was becoming a friend, but I still didn't know her well enough to open up completely. Erin was off on an expedition, leading a group of rafters on a trip down the New River in West Virginia. I'd met her the first time I'd tried a kayak at her business, and there was definitely a spark between us, but that didn't mean I could bare my soul to her just yet, either. That left my mechanic and friend Wayne, but he was giving all of his attention lately to the new lady in his life. Though I'd acquired an entire new roster of friends with the addition of River's Edge to my life, there really was no one around I could talk to.

The stars, at least for the moment, had lost their pull for me, and the cold, biting wind just reinforced the fact that I was alone. I put the chair and blanket away feeling the chill of the night, and headed down to my apartment. Once I was back in the warmth, the flashing light of the answering machine caught my eye again, and I knew I'd have to sift through the messages before I'd be able to get to sleep that night. Curiosity was a curse of mine, one I'd had no luck breaking in the past. The light now read twenty-eight; someone must have called while I'd been up on the roof.

Most of the messages were as I'd expected—people calling demanding to know if I'd really killed Gretel, reporters asking for interviews and a few folks even defending my honor—but the last message struck me as the oddest of the lot.

"Candles soon burn out," was all the caller said in a whispered, gravelly voice.

Now what in the world did that mean? Was somebody trying to be funny, or was it some kind of veiled threat? I reached to hit the save button so I could replay it for the sheriff, but my finger slipped off it and hit the delete key instead; so much for preserving it for further study. Why would anyone threaten me like that? It was a little too creepy for my taste. I wished I'd saved it for Morton to hear, but now I couldn't even mention it to him. Knowing the sheriff, he'd probably think my accidental erasure was just a little too convenient, since I couldn't back the claim up with anything other than my word. If any of the other messages I'd accidentally deleted were important, I just had to hope that they'd call back when they didn't hear from me.

As I tried to sleep, my thoughts kept returning to what tomorrow would bring. I couldn't get comfortable in my bed as my mind raced back to the unwelcome sight of

Gretel collapsing, slow motion, over and over again. I was almost ready to give up on sleep when it came unexpectedly.

I might have been better off staying awake. All night the reel kept playing over and over again in my mind, and I was in no shape to face the day when my alarm finally went off.

I'D PREPARED MYSELF to face a mob at the candleshop, but twenty minutes before opening, there wasn't a soul in sight, including Eve. I'd skipped my ritual breakfast at The Crocked Pot, not wanting to face any strangers I didn't have to. Instead, I'd heated a few frozen waffles upstairs and lingered in the apartment, puttering around as the time crept by before finally heading down to At Wick's End. It was Sunday, and we didn't open until noon, so I had a lot of time to kill. Ordinarily I'd take my kayak out on the water—regardless of the cold— or go for a walk, or even go down to the candleshop and practice some new technique, but I was in no mood for any of my options.

Though it was nearly eleven when I finally stepped outside for the first time that day, the weather had turned back to the cold we normally expected for late fall in our part of North Carolina, and I was glad for my jacket even in my brief commute from my apartment upstairs to the candleshop below.

As I hung my coat up in the office, I glanced at the schedule and realized that Eve wasn't due to come in at all that day. It looked like I was going to have to face the crowds alone. As I busied myself preparing to open the store, the telephone started to ring, but I wasn't about to answer it until I had to. Unfortunately, by noon it still hadn't given up, and it was time to unlock the doors.

Bracing myself, I walked to the door and pulled the blinds back.

No one was there.

I opened the door with more relief than I should have felt and peeked outside. Not a solitary soul was loitering anywhere nearby. While I was happy none of the pests from the day before had shown up, the fact that none of my regular customers were there either took the edge off my temporary joy. Sunday was normally a big day for us, but it was looking bleak from the start. So was this going to be it? Would Gretel manage to carry out her threat in death, to bury me and my candleshop?

The ringing telephone pulled me back into the shop, and my hand shook as I answered it.

"At Wick's End," I said.

"Harrison Black, I was worried something had happened to you. I've been calling since ten thirty."

"Hi, Eve. I'm here."

I could hear her take a deep breath, then she said, "Harrison, I realize I'm not scheduled to work today, but I don't think you should be alone. Are you crushed with people today?"

I looked around the empty shop. "It's nothing I can't handle."

"Don't put up a brave front for me, I know how overwhelming it was yesterday. I'm coming in."

It was time to come clean. "Eve, there's not a soul in sight. It looks like we're already yesterday's news."

She hesitated, then said, "Oh dear, I was afraid of that, too. I gather you haven't read *The Gunpowder Gazette* yet."

"I forgot all about it. How bad is it?"

"They didn't overtly name you as the killer, but they did

everything else. I'm afraid it's quite nasty in its quiet little way."

I let out a heavy sigh. "Well, at least that explains why I'm by myself. I'm going to go over to Millie's and buy a newspaper."

"I wouldn't if I were you."

I shrugged. "If they are going to be lying about me, I want to know what they're saying."

"Would you like me to come in, if nothing else, for moral support?"

"No, but thanks for asking. I'll need you tomorrow for a full day, at least if Mrs. Jorgenson keeps her lesson. Enjoy today off. I know I would."

"Harrison, ordinarily I'd never suggest this, but you could just close the candleshop for a few days until things calm down."

"Eve, this isn't going to blow over, and I'm not going to hide or run away. I didn't do anything. I'm going to be right here at the candleshop, where I belong."

"Suit yourself," she said. "If you change your mind, call me and I'll be right in."

"Don't wait by the phone. As it is, it looks like I'll be getting a lot of dusting done."

After we hung up, I changed my mind about grabbing a newspaper. Did I really want to put myself through that? I decided I could sit around and mope all afternoon or I could actually be productive, so I grabbed a duster and started in on the shelves. Two hours later the place was as clean as it ever had been since I'd taken over, and not a single person had darkened my doorway. I was about to give up entirely when I heard the bell over the front door ring. At that point, I was willing to answer a reporter's questions if it meant a sale for the store.

It was Sanora, the potter from River's Edge.

"Did you come by for the wake?" I asked her.

"Surely they're not having it here," she said.

"I'm talking about the one for the candleshop," I said. "Hey, who's watching The Pot Shot?"

"I never opened. I'm going to start closing the shop on Sundays and Mondays during the winter. I figure I work so hard during the summer months, I deserve a break now and then. You should do it."

I gestured around the empty shop. "I'm afraid if I did that, nobody would notice."

"That bad, is it? Things will get better, Harrison, you have to rely on that."

I shrugged. Given the evidence, I couldn't make myself believe anything of the sort. "So what brings you here?"

"I came by to see if you wanted to play hooky with me."

"I'm not in the mood for playing," I said, "but thanks for offering."

"Are you sure? I'm heading up to the Blue Ridge Parkway. It's a beautiful day for a drive."

"I really can't. Besides, I'm afraid I wouldn't be very good company today."

She frowned, then said, "Tell you what, I'll give you a rain check, and we'll do it some other time."

"Thanks, I appreciate that," I said.

Over the next few hours, Heather, Millie and Suzanne Gladstone from the new antique shop all popped in to try to cheer me up, and though I appreciated their efforts, it was all wasted on me. When I closed up at six, it was a first for me, and hopefully a last, too.

I hadn't sold a single thing all day.

As I locked the front door, I realized the only two people associated with River's Edge who hadn't checked on me were Gary Cragg and Pearly Gray. Cragg wouldn't visit me on a Sunday if I was giving away hundred-dollar bills, but it was so out of character for Pearly not to offer his support that I found myself worrying about my handyman and friend. Did he hold me responsible in any way for what had happened to Gretel? Or was he off mourning on his own? Either way, I wished I could talk to him, but Pearly was so adamant about keeping his privacy in his off-hours that I didn't even know where he lived, and in a town as small as Micah's Ridge, that was saying something. There was no doubt in my mind I could track him down if I had to—I'd been there long enough to know who to ask—but I figured I'd better respect his wishes. If and when he was ready to talk, he knew where to find me.

PACING AROUND MY apartment that night, I debated calling Heather to see if I could host her cat, Esmeralda, at my place for the next few days. Though I'd never admit it to anyone, being the feline's designated roommate whenever Heather was away had become an important part of my life at River's Edge. I'd developed a bond with Esme that had surprised me greatly, since she was the first cat I'd ever warmed up to. Heather had offered to set me up with a cat of my own, but I was afraid my affection didn't extend to the whole species, just that one particular cat, as cantankerous as she could be at times. I started for the roof a dozen times, but the thought of being high above the world right now wasn't a pleasant one.

There were only so many steps I could take in my apartment before I started wearing a path in the floor, so I decided to go out. What was the worst that could happen? Well, people could point and stare; they could call me a murderer, or throw rocks at me. Still, I was willing to chance it. I grabbed a baseball cap on my way out and pulled it down low over my eyes. It wouldn't fool anyone who knew me, but hopefully it would distract everyone else.

I was startled to find Becka approaching the building as I walked out. "Bad timing, I'm just on my way out," I said, trying to manage a smile for her.

"I'm so sorry I couldn't get here sooner. Harrison, I can't believe this is happening to you."

"Thanks, I appreciate that." The last thing I wanted to discuss with Becka was my innocence. "Have you had any more problems with your stalker?"

"Don't call him that, it gives me the creeps," she said. "No, I haven't seen him since I was here. I'm hoping he's given up on me. Harrison, what are you going to do?"

"If he's not bothering you, there's not really anything I can do, is there?"

She touched my arm lightly. "I'm not talking about me; I'm talking about you."

"I'm going to trust Morton to find Gretel's killer, Becka. There's not much I can do on my own."

She rubbed my arm gently, then started up toward my shoulder when I pulled away. "Listen, I appreciate you coming by, but I'm fine, honest. Like I said, I was just on my way out."

I could tell she was waiting for an invitation to join me, but I wanted to be alone. Even if I'd been looking for company, I most likely wouldn't have turned to my ex-girlfriend.

I expected a heated protest from her, but Becka said, "I understand. If you need anything, even if it's just someone to listen, call me."

"Thanks," I said. She got into her car and drove off, and I headed to the parking behind River's Edge.

I got in Belle's Ford truck and started driving around Micah's Ridge, happy for once that night had fallen so early. Usually the winter months depressed me, especially those after Christmas. We'd done well over the holiday season, and I'd wondered what I was going to do with our growing cash reserves. I was glad I'd fought the impulse to squander it on a trip. I'd need every dime I'd banked if things kept going like they were headed. I slowed the truck near A Slice of Heaven—my favorite pizza place in the world—and debated going in. But though I'd felt brave leaving my apartment, I wasn't ready to throw myself into the thick of humanity, not with the suspicions that were hanging over me. Maybe coming out wasn't that great an idea after all. It was starting to rain, and my windshield was streaked with moisture as I turned my wipers on. I started back for River's Edge and was nearly there when I heard a police siren behind me. I looked in my rearview mirror with a sinking feeling in my stomach. A police car was on my tail. What had I done? Had I sped through a stoplight, lost in my thoughts? I pulled over onto the shoulder and could see the officer get out and start toward me.

I rolled down the window and saw Sheriff Morton approach. Before he could say a word, I said, "I'm sorry, I didn't realize I'd done anything wrong."

"This isn't about your driving, Harrison. You've got bigger problems than that."

"What is it? You're not going to arrest me, are you?"

"Quit asking me that. You'll know it if I'm going to lock you up. Listen, we're almost back to the candleshop. I'll follow you and we can talk there."

I did as I was told, my thoughts racing as I tried to figure out exactly what I'd done now. I'd know soon enough, but that didn't keep me from guessing.

I parked in front of the candleshop instead of in the alley behind River's Edge, and the sheriff pulled up beside me a minute later. I asked, "So what's going on?"

"Inside," he said as he gestured to the door. The rain was really starting to intensify.

The automatic security lights—armed with motion detectors—turned on as I approached the shop, and I thought about when Pearly and I had installed them. I flipped the lights on as I walked into At Wick's End, but the sheriff hadn't followed me. He'd evidently ducked back into his squad car and was talking on his radio. Without a word or a glance back at me, he pulled out of the parking lot, his lights coming on as he did. Whatever he'd wanted to talk to me about had been overruled by something else.

I waited around half an hour, but for the first time in months, being in the candleshop was depressing. Not even the brightly decorated wax candles on display could cheer me up. I locked the shop's front door and headed upstairs. My dinner matched my mood: a cold sandwich, some stale potato chips and a two-liter bottle of root beer that had gone flat days ago. It wasn't exactly a gourmet meal, but I choked it down.

I didn't bother with a plate, eating off a paper towel instead. It sure made doing the dishes easy. Looking through my books, I settled on a biography of Thomas Jefferson. As much as I loved reading mysteries, I was in no mood for dead bodies, not after the night I'd spent replaying Gretel's murder in my sleep.

There was a pounding on my door as I picked the book up, so I laid it down on the table and opened the door.

It was the sheriff, and he was dripping wet. "Sorry about that," he said. "I had a call I needed to take." He started in, then said, "Tell you what; why don't we do this in your shop? I don't want to get your floor wet in there."

I nodded. "I wish I knew what this was about."

"Just be patient for another minute," he said.

"Let me grab my keys and I'll meet you downstairs." I picked up my key ring and locked the apartment behind me. Morton was under the awning in front of the candleshop waiting for me.

I unlocked the door yet again and flipped on the lights. I was spending more time there when I was closed than when I'd been open.

After he walked in, I locked the door behind him. "So what's going on?"

He pulled something out of his pocket, and I could see a letter in a clear plastic envelope. It said, I SAW THE CANDLE GUY KILL HER, in block letters.

"You call this evidence?" I said. "I know who did this."

"I didn't say I believed it, I just thought you should know what you're facing here. And I highly doubt you know the sender. There wasn't an identifying mark on it, and it was mailed from the downtown post office in Micah's Ridge."

"Some nutcase was waiting for me by my truck yesterday. He told me that for the right price, he would swear he saw someone else kill Gretel. When I ran him off, he threatened me with something just like this. I never thought he'd follow through with it, though."

"How did he threaten you?"

"He said that he could just as easily tell the police that he'd seen me shoot her instead of backing me up."

Morton shook his head. "Harrison, I hate to break it to you, but we've gotten several tips from people claiming that you're the one who shot Gretel."

"Did anybody leave their name and number?" I asked.

That actually got a smile from the sheriff. "No, it's funny how brave folks are when it's all anonymous, isn't it? You're taking the newspaper write-up pretty well."

"That's because I didn't read it," I said.

"You probably should, just to know what they're saying about you."

"I don't need to. I'm already expecting the worst."

"Maybe you're right," he said. "The real reason I came by was to tell you to watch your back. There's a witch hunt brewing, and I won't have it in my jurisdiction."

"So you believe me?" I asked.

"Let's just say I'm not rushing to judgment," he said. "On the face of it, I'd say it wasn't your style to shoot a woman in the back like that."

"Thanks for that, anyway," I said.

Morton headed for the door, then waited for me to let him out. As I shut off the lights, I said, "Sheriff, thanks for the warning. I appreciate it."

"Just thought you ought to know."

I went back upstairs, picked up the biography and started to read, but I just couldn't get into it. I drifted off wondering how many accusations tomorrow would bring.

Six

I discovered that some kind citizen had left me two newspapers in front of the candleshop when I went downstairs the next morning. They'd thoughtfully provided yesterday's edition of *The Gunpowder Gazette,* along with Monday's paper as well. I considered tossing them in the recycling without reading them, but my curiosity got the better of me, and after going inside, I unfolded the papers with dread.

It was even worse than I'd expected.

CANDLEMAKER SLAIN AT FAIR, the headline screamed across the top of page one of Sunday's paper. The top of the fold carried the story, along with a glamour shot Gretel had used for publicity announcing the opening of Flickering Lights. When I flipped the paper over, I was shocked to find my own face staring back. The tag line under it said, *"Harrison Black, rival candlemaker, questioned at the scene."* It wasn't the most flattering photo I'd ever seen of myself, and somehow they'd managed to shade it two tones darker than normal, giving me a dark and sinister look. If that was how they'd handled the photograph, I couldn't imagine what the article itself said. I scanned it for my name and found it uncomfortably close to the top. *Harrison Black, embroiled in a heated rivalry with the victim, was present at the scene of the crime. Though Mr. Black was questioned extensively by the police, he was released due to insufficient evidence. An anonymous source with the police department said that though there was an eyewitness to the slaying, there was no other specific direct evidence against Mr. Black at the time of his questioning.* That was just wonderful. Reading the article, I was starting to get the suspicion that I'd done it myself.

The follow-up paper wasn't much better, but at least there were no photographs of me in it. Instead, there was a small headline below the fold that said the police were close to an arrest. I was startled to see that it also mentioned several anonymous tips the police had received, and that they'd even noted Sheriff Morton's visit to River's Edge the night before! It was obvious someone had been watching the candleshop last night.

Eve came in and found me reading the paper. "Honestly, Harrison, don't you have anything better to do with your time than read that rag?"

"I didn't buy it. Someone left it on our doorstep. Did you see this?" I asked, waving the paper around in the air.

"I don't read rubbish," she said, "And you shouldn't, either. Don't you have a class to prepare for?"

"Do you honestly think she's coming?" Mrs. Jorgenson was strong willed and tough minded, but I couldn't believe she'd show up after all the bad publicity I was getting lately.

"Come, Harrison, she's too devoted to candlemaking to believe these lies. She'll be here."

"Then I'd better get ready for her, just in case she shows up," I said.

I started pulling the supplies we would need for our next lesson. We'd already covered candles rolled from beeswax sheets, and touched on dipping candles, too. Now it was time to pour, something I'd been practicing quite a bit on my own and was most eager to start teaching.

Eve came back as I was setting the worktables up in the classroom for our lesson. From the look on her face, she was bearing more bad news.

"What is it?"

"Mrs. Jorgenson called. She's not going to be able to make it."

I slammed a block of wax down on the table. "Why am I not surprised?"

"Harrison, she had a meeting she forgot all about, and you know how she loves those things."

As I gathered the materials back together, I said, "So if she really wanted to be here, when did she reschedule her next class for?"

When Eve didn't answer, I pushed her. "Well?"

"She said she'd let us know."

"Yeah, right." I brushed past Eve and said, "We gave it our best shot, didn't we?"

"Harrison Black, we're not out of this yet."

"Face it, the ship is sinking, and we're both going down with it."

Eve frowned, started to say something, then changed her mind as she headed for the front.

I asked her, "Where are you going?"

"We're still open for business, Harrison. I'm going to go unlock the door."

I let her go, lost in my own self-pity. My worst fear had come true: Mrs. Jorgenson had abandoned us, cutting the last vestiges of profitability we had. I'd have to speak with Mary Ann, my bookkeeper, and see how much of a cushion we had before it was time to print up the GOING OUT OF BUSINESS signs.

When I walked up front to find her number, Eve was actually waiting on a customer. The woman looked familiar to me, but I didn't recognize her immediately. She had frosted hair piled on her head in some kind of complicated structure that defied gravity, no doubt with the aid of a full can of hairspray. As Eve rang up her sale, I said, "It's good to see you here again."

"I've never been in this shop in my life," she said, avoiding eye contact with me. "I just found out about this place this morning."

"I'm sorry, but haven't we met before?"

"No, I'm sure you're mistaken. I'm new to the area." She grabbed her change from Eve, nearly forgot her bag, then retrieved it and bolted out of the shop.

"What was that all about?" I asked. "Another faithful reader of *The Gunpowder Gazette*?"

"No, at least she never mentioned it. She told me she just moved down from Charleston, West Virginia. Harrison, you really should try harder to remember our customers. Belle was an expert at it."

"Come on, Eve, I can't remember every single person who comes in the door." I looked around the shop. "Until lately, that is. I'm telling you, that woman looked familiar. If I didn't see her in here, where did I see her?"

"I do hope that's a rhetorical question," Eve said. "I certainly can't help you with it."

"It'll come to me. Just give me some time to think about it."

She frowned, then said, "In the meantime, you really should speak with Mary Ann about our situation. It might be prudent to find out where we stand financially. Not that I'm trying to tell you how to run the business."

"I was just thinking the same thing myself. I've been meaning to give her a call."

I couldn't bring myself to dial Mary Ann's number. I was serious about seeing what kind of slump we could handle before things got really desperate, but the phone call would have to wait. Pearly Gray walked into At Wick's End, and from the look on his face, he'd just lost his last friend in the world.

Pearly said, "Harrison, do you have a moment?"

"I do for you. Come on back to the office."

He said, "I hate to ask, but could we speak outside?"

"No problem." I would have gone to the zoo with him if it would make him feel better. "Eve, I'll be back."

"That's fine," she said, carefully avoiding Pearly's glance. The two of them had gone out a few times, until Eve had discovered that Pearly was escorting several different women around town. Since then, they had been going through a rather chilly exchange of insincere pleasantries.

I walked outside the candleshop with Pearly and asked, "So where would you like to talk? We can take Belle's truck somewhere."

"That won't be necessary," he said. "The steps here will be fine."

I followed him down the concrete steps in front of River's Edge that led to the Gunpowder River, and we sat three levels from the water's edge. It was nearly as good as the tailgate of a truck for talking. Most Southern men didn't like a lot of eye contact when they talked to each other, and any pretense to avoid it was acceptable.

As he stared out over the water, Pearly said, "Harrison,

I owe you so many apologies I don't even know where to begin."

"My friend, you don't owe me anything. You come here every day and do a fine job keeping River's Edge afloat. It's all I have any right to expect of you."

"You said it yourself, though. We've become friends since your great-aunt died. And a friend owes you more than an employee does. I should have told you from the beginning that I was keeping company with Gretel. In my defense, I didn't know that she'd planned to open a candleshop until she'd already bought the place. The fool woman paid cash for the building *and* her franchising fee, if you can imagine that."

"She wasn't just renting? I can't believe she owned the space outright." I was more than a little jealous. If I lived to be eighty, I might own River's Edge, but that depended on a lot of good luck to happen along the way.

"She got some kind of incredible inheritance when her parents died. Her brother squandered his, but Gretel had a knack for making her portion grow. They ended up hating each other because of it. It bothered me at first, knowing how much she was worth, but Gretel never put on airs about it. I'm doing this badly," he added with a heavy sigh.

"You're doing fine," I said. Though I knew Pearly's history as a psychologist, I also realized that professional relationships and personal ones were quite different. While I never doubted for an instant that he had been good at his job, I knew it was difficult for most people to apologize.

"Don't be so sure. There's more I haven't told you yet. I'm afraid she got the idea for her shop from me, at least indirectly. I was bragging about what a fine job you've been doing here, and she started to ask questions. I thought she was just taking an interest in my life, but it turns out she was mining me for information. I probably should have walked away after that, but blast it all, it's been difficult for me to find a woman who challenged me like she did."

"Nobody has the right to expect that kind of loyalty in their friendship. You followed your heart, Pearly."

"You're being too easy on me, Harrison. She thought River's Edge was coming between us, and I'm afraid she started to resent you. She told me she was going to wipe you out, so I broke it off with her."

"When did all this happen?"

"The night before she was murdered," Pearly said, his voice nearly choking. "I was at the fair to make amends— to see if we couldn't work out some kind of compromise— but it took me too long to work up my nerve, and by the time I was ready to talk to her, she was dead."

I couldn't imagine what he was going through. His unresolved issues with her would probably haunt him the rest of his life, and I didn't envy Pearly that at all. And to think I'd called my troubled sleep nightmares!

"I'm sorry if I played any part in your grief, Pearly."

"I'll work it out, Harrison. I have to find a way to live with what happened. The first step is making things right with you."

"We're fine, Pearly. If you need someone to talk to, I'm right here."

He nodded, then we both stood. As he offered me his hand, Pearly said, "I appreciate the offer, but what I really need right now is a few days away to clear my head. Would that be all right with you? I'd like to go up into the mountains alone and sort this out."

I could hardly deny his request. "Take as much time as you need."

"You're a good friend, Harrison, better than I have any right to expect."

"I have my moments," I said, smiling slightly.

Pearly left, the slump in his shoulders eased somewhat. I couldn't imagine what he was going through, but I'd do my best to help him deal with it. I'd find a way to hold the complex together until he got back.

It was too early for lunch, but I couldn't face going back to an empty shop, so I decided to indulge in one of Millie's pastry treats. She waited on a few customers ahead of me, then said, "What can I get you today, Harrison?"

"I was hoping you had something special on the menu this morning."

She smiled. "You mean something along the lines of a bakery item?"

"I wouldn't say no to something sweet," I said.

"I've got just the thing, if you can wait five minutes. It's cooling on the rack. It's called Apple Pan Dowdy and it's wonderful, if I say so myself. I got the recipe from George's mother, though she put off giving it to me until we'd been married ten years. She wanted to make sure the marriage was going to last before she shared the family secret; it's that good."

"I can't wait," I said.

"Well, you're going to have to force yourself. It's so much better when it's cooled slightly." She lowered her voice, though most of her customers had taken the tables near the windows to enjoy the river view. "How are you?"

"Well, I was hoping it was just my imagination, but if things keep going the way they are, I'm going to be out of the candleshop business by spring."

"Harrison, you've got to have more faith in people than that. Your customers are going to stick by you."

I considered telling her about Mrs. Jorgenson's cancellation, and the feeble excuse she'd used, but there was no reason to burden Millie with my problems. "Yeah, you're probably right."

"That's the spirit." Her telephone rang, and as she answered it, I looked through the display case to see what else Millie had been up to. Though she was trying to keep her voice low, I could catch everything she was saying. "I won't do it, George, so stop asking." After a pause, she said, "I don't care what they think, and frankly, I'm disappointed you do. Good-bye, George."

Millie hung up the telephone rather forcefully, then stared at me a moment. "Don't pretend you didn't hear that," she said.

"It's none of my business," I said.

"That's where you're wrong. Some of the folks George works with think I should take a vacation until this mess is cleared up, and my loving husband, who's normally bright enough to know better, suggested I do just that."

"Millie, I'm sorry. I can't believe this is affecting you."

"We're a family here, Harrison. What affects one of us affects the rest. Don't you worry, I'm not going anywhere."

"Thanks, I appreciate that."

Millie said, "In fact, I can do you one better than that. I made an extra Pan Dowdy for George, but he's shown himself particularly unworthy at the moment. I want you to have it; if you like the recipe, that is."

"I shouldn't," I said, thinking of the calories more than anything else.

"Nonsense, you'll hurt my feelings if you turn it down. It's either you or George eating this. Otherwise it's going in the garbage."

A man from one of the tables said, "If they don't want it, I'll pay top dollar, Millie. I've had your Pan Dowdy before."

"Harry James Hickman, you know better than to eavesdrop on other folks while they're talking." Then she winked at him and added, "But I might save you a piece if you play your cards right."

"Yes, Ma'am," Harry said with a smile.

"Would it help if I talked to George myself?" I said. "Maybe I can convince him that I didn't do anything wrong."

Millie shook her head. "Thanks for the offer, but I'm sure he'll realize his error by the time he gets home, especially after he misses the smell of my cooking. He doesn't know it yet, but George is taking me out to dinner tonight."

I was about to reply when Suzanne Gladstone rushed in. She made straight for me and said, "Harrison, I need Pearly, and I need him fast."

"I'm sorry, but he's taking a few days off."

"I'm sorry too, more than I can tell you. What am I supposed to do? I've got a leak in my bathroom pipes."

"I'll take a look and see what I can do," I said, not all that confident I could help.

Millie said, "Don't forget to come back here for your treat after you're finished."

"I'll be back as soon as I can." Plumbing was definitely not my favorite thing to do, but I'd been a camp counselor during three summers in college and I'd learned to take a stab at just about anything. If worse came to worse and it was something I couldn't fix, I'd call a plumber, though I could ill afford the expense. As I followed Suzanne to her shop, I found myself hoping that my handyman figured things out quickly enough to get back to help keep River's Edge afloat.

Seven

"I didn't know you were a repairman, too," Suzanne Gladstone said as I searched under the sink for the cause of her leak.

"I'm not making any claims, but I'll have to do until Pearly gets back." The vanity in the store's bathroom had a bucket inside to capture the leak, and I was glad that whoever had converted River's Edge from a factory to stores and shops had put individual water cutoffs in each space. At least that way I wouldn't have to shut everyone's water off to fix one leak. I peered under the sink before doing that, though. I needed to see where the water was coming from before I could fix it.

"So how do you like being at River's Edge?" I asked as I removed the bucket.

"It's certainly different from a stand-alone store. That's what I'm used to. You've got quite an unusual assortment of tenants, don't you? No, that doesn't sound right. What I should have said was eclectic."

"I'll take either one," I said as I spotted the leak. Water was seeping through the connection between the cold water supply line and the faucet. Gladly, it was something I could fix. I took the adjustable wrench I'd picked up on the way over to her shop and gave the nut a quick quarter turn, making it snug again. The water stopped, and I pronounced it fixed.

"My, that's wonderful," she said. "Why do you need Pearly if you're so good at this?"

"Believe me, I got lucky this time. I couldn't run River's Edge without Pearly Gray."

I emptied the bucket into the drain, then handed it back to her. "There you go. Good as new."

"Harrison," she said. "I don't mean to butt in, but what are you going to do about that woman's murder?"

"What can I do?" I asked. "The police are looking into it."

"Is that good enough?" she asked, then quickly added, "I know it's none of my business, but I can't help myself. You can't just let your candleshop die. I had a friend in Western Mississippi who was accused by her boss of stealing, though she never took a dime. No charges were ever filed and there was never a hint of proof, but she couldn't get a job in her field anywhere in town because of the rumors. First there were whispers, and then folks were saying things out loud. She had to move to Tupelo, where nobody knew her, and start over. Don't let that happen to you."

"Thanks, Suzanne, I appreciate your support."

"That's what friends are for, Harrison. Think about what I said."

"I will," I promised. I returned the wrench to Pearly's small workroom and logged in the repair in his ledger.

Pearly was the most organized handyman I'd ever come

across in my life, keeping track of every call he made at River's Edge. I wrote down the date, time and nature of the repair, proud to be able to add my own entry. I scanned the listings before mine, wondering what Pearly had handled while I'd been holed up licking my wounds.

Something odd struck me as I saw Sanora's name listed; the times logged between the initial complaint and the actual repair were spaced seven hours apart, though there were no other problems that day. I glanced through the log and saw that none of the other repairs had taken more than half an hour to get to in the last month of the journal. The gap had been registered the day before the fair, and I wondered where Pearly had slipped off to for most of the day.

Was I being paranoid, as Eve often accused me? Surely if Pearly had something to hide, he would have doctored the entry to escape notice. Still, the gap left me uneasy, not because of his response time, but because it was so out of character. Could that have been when Pearly was breaking up with Gretel? The worst thing was I couldn't even ask him about it, not unless I had more reason than a logged entry to suspect he was up to no good. Pearly would take the questioning as an affront, and I couldn't blame him.

As I washed my hands, I remembered the promised baked treat, and Millie had it waiting for me when I walked back in.

I held the pan to my nose. "It smells heavenly."

She handed me a fork. "It's the perfect temperature right now. You've got to try it and tell me what you think."

It was all the prodding I needed. I took a bite of the brown topping, then dug into the softened apples below it. The juice from baking had been soaked into the cake-like crust, a mixture of sensations that burst in my mouth.

"This is unbelievable."

Millie smiled. "I thought you'd like it. Take the rest back with you; it saves beautifully in the refrigerator."

"It won't last long enough for that," I said, then I thanked her again.

As I walked back to my candleshop, I kept thinking about what Suzanne had said. She was right, whether I cared to admit it or not. I couldn't stand idly by and watch the business Belle had worked so hard to build crumble into dust, nor could I afford to wait for the sheriff to name the killer. He had more time than I did.

I needed to do something, and I needed to do it soon.

"JUBAL, I WAS wondering if I could talk to you for a minute."

Eve hadn't minded me leaving the candleshop at all. I'd told her I had a few errands to run, but there was no doubt she knew what I was up to, and it was equally clear she didn't approve of my behavior. That was just too bad. Though her livelihood was on the line as well, At Wick's End wasn't her business; it was mine. I'd stashed what little was left of the Pan Dowdy upstairs in my refrigerator, then after checking in with her, I'd headed into town.

Jubal offered a sad smile. "Harrison, of course I have time for you. Just let me ring up the next few customers and I'm all yours."

Three of the folks who had been shopping at Flickering Lights had been recent regular customers at my candleshop, and when they spotted me coming in, they'd scurried away without buying anything, ducking out as quickly as they could. It was what I'd suspected, but it still didn't make it any easier seeing them shopping at my competitor's store and not mine. At least Mrs. Jorgenson wasn't there. If she'd switched alliances, I'd rather not know about it. I browsed around the candleshop and was surprised to find the shelf stock running low or even completely out in some cases. I hated to think what that meant to my business if Jubal couldn't even keep his inventory stocked.

Once we were alone, I said, "Sorry about that. I didn't mean to run any of your customers off."

Jubal shook his head. "So that's what that was all about. I wondered. Harrison, I feel guilty thriving because of your misfortune. I'm not even sure candlemaking is a good fit for me, though Gretel seemed to be quite taken with it."

"I thought you said you were excited about coming here and doing this?"

"Being near my cousin was more the reason for my interest than any genuine affection for the trade. I suppose I'll run it for the interim, at least until her brother shows up. If they ever manage to track Hans down, that is."

"Have you spoken with Gretel's lawyer about the disposition of her things?"

Jubal said, "A tired old man came by this morning with some papers, but he was summoned back to his office before he had the opportunity to tell me anything. We have another appointment this evening after my regular business hours are finished here."

A woman came in, plopped a large forest green candle in the shape of a pinecone on the sales table and said, "There's something wrong with this candle you sold me. I can't get it to light."

Jubal raised an eyebrow, and without a word he flicked a lighter open with his left hand and lit the scorched wick. It sputtered for a few seconds, then as the heat touched the wax, the candle glowed in a steady light.

"Why wouldn't it do that for me?" she asked.

Jubal said, "Sometimes it takes a steady flame. Is there anything else?"

She frowned, obviously ready for more of a fight, then blew out the flame and stormed back out.

After she was gone, Jubal said, "Some folks are just looking for a reason to be angry, aren't they?"

"It takes all kinds," I agreed.

Jubal stood from his place behind the register, stretched for a second, then said, "Enough about my worries. What brings you here?"

"I wanted to ask you if you've been able to come up with anybody else who could have wished Gretel ill."

Jubal paused, then said, "You know, I've been debating calling you. I thought of something, or someone rather, but I wasn't sure I should say anything. It's certainly not enough to bother the police with."

"Why don't you tell me, and then we'll decide how important it is together."

Jubal shrugged. "Very well. A man named Runion was pressuring Gretel about the shop a few days before she was killed."

"Greg Runion?"

"I think that was his name. Do you know him?"

I nodded. "He was nosing around River's Edge before I told him the place wasn't for sale. It doesn't make sense why Runion would be after this place. No offense, but it's just one shop. I thought he went after bigger game."

Jubal waved a hand in the air. "I told you it was probably nothing. How's Pearly doing?"

"He's taking it pretty hard. I gave him some time off to clear his head. He's heading up to the mountains."

Jubal nodded. "I know they were having problems. I just wish . . ."

"What?" I asked.

"I wish they'd been on speaking terms when this happened. Pearly shouldn't have to deal with the guilt, too."

"He'll be all right. The man's made of stern stock."

"I must admit," Jubal said, "I'm feeling guilty myself. I keep thinking that if I'd been there with Gretel, I might have seen what was about to happen and stop it somehow."

"Don't be too hard on yourself. Somebody had to stay here and run the shop. I had my assistant open At Wick's End, too."

Jubal frowned. "I didn't even get a lunch break that day; I wolfed down a bagel behind the counter between customers. In fact, I didn't get any sort of respite until the police called me with the news."

A customer walked in—not one of mine, I was glad to see—and asked about gel candle kits. Jubal said to me, "Sorry, I need to handle this. Harrison, if there's anything I can do, all you have to do is ask."

"Thanks. The same goes for you."

I left Jubal to his customer, hoping Eve was keeping busy as well, and took off in search of Greg Runion. Why would he be after Flickering Lights? If he'd wanted the candleshop location, he would have been able to buy it long before Gretel purchased the building. I wasn't a big fan of the man, so I was going to have to squelch my natural tendency toward him if I was going to get anything out of him.

Runion's secretary, a leggy brunette with a ready smile, greeted me as I walked in the door of Runion Developments. "May I help you?" she said in a Tennessee accent I've always been a sucker for. Folks from different parts of the country mostly heard a Southern accent as one dialect, but I'd been born and raised in the South, and I could tell Tennessee from the Carolinas, Georgia from Alabama. Each region had its own unique twang, and there was nothing sweeter to my ears than the sound of a woman from Tennessee. It didn't help matters that nearly every woman I'd ever met from that particular state had broken my heart at least once.

"Knoxville, right?" I said with a smile.

"I grew up ten miles outside the city limits. You're good."

"I do party tricks too," I said. "Is Mr. Runion around?"

She looked at his schedule, then frowned. "Is he expecting you? I'm afraid I don't have any openings till next week."

"I think he'll want to talk to me." That was a stretch, but I needed to get past her somehow.

She picked up the telephone and asked, "Whom may I say is calling?"

"Tell him it's Harrison Black from River's Edge."

She whispered something into the phone, then said to me, "He'll be right with you."

Before she could hang up, Runion came out, cool gray eyes peering out below large black eyebrows. Runion had played football for Micah's Ridge, had won them their only county title before fading fast at Carolina. He'd come back to town a hero, then gone into the insurance business before heading into real estate. I hadn't grown up in Micah's Ridge, so I hadn't known his history until he'd carefully worked it all into our first conversation. Every third thing out of the man's mouth was a lie, so I wondered how much of what he said I could believe.

"Harrison, it's nice of you to drop by. I've only got a few minutes—something urgent has come up—but I'll give you what time I've got." He turned to his secretary and said, "Jeanie, get Hardin on the line in four, then buzz me."

I walked back into his office and saw Runion's dream

projects decorating his walls. They were all artist's rendi-
tions, since none of them had actually come to fruition.

"So," he said, "are we ready to work out some kind of
deal on River's Edge? I wish I could offer you the same
thing we discussed before, but I'll have to drop my offer
by twenty percent. Times change."

I smiled, but there was no warmth in it. "If anything, the
property's more valuable now than it was before."

Runion frowned. "Playing hardball, huh? I might be
able to come within five percent of my last offer, but no
more."

I ignored his counteroffer, especially since I had no intention of selling River's Edge. "I heard you were interested in Gretel Barnett's place."

"Now who told you that?"

"You're not the only one with contacts around Micah's
Ridge. Somebody told me you were pushing her pretty
hard."

Runion held up his hands. "Your source has been lying
to you. As a matter of fact, a man called me offering the
property last week. Nothing came of it, though. It turns out
the place wasn't his to sell."

"Who'd you talk to?"

"I didn't get his name, but when I called Ms. Barnett to
follow up, she told me she had no intention of leaving the
area. Some crank was having his jollies at my expense,
most likely. Now what about River's Edge?"

I was suddenly tired of the conversation. "You want to
know the truth? I just don't feel good about selling the
place."

Runion said, "Come on, everything's for sale, if the
price is right." He pointed toward the front office. "Did
you see Jeanie out there? She kept saying no to me, too,
until I finally wore her down."

I shook my head. "Sorry, it's not going to happen."

I walked out of his office and looked at the secretary. Evidently I wasn't too successful in hiding my disappointment in what Runion had just told me about her.

She started to say good-bye, then her smile faded as she said, "He's been bragging about me again, hasn't he?"

I bit my lip, then said, "I was hoping you were a better judge of character than that. Not that it's any of my business."

Without another word to me, she stood up and stormed into his office. "Gregory Runion, if you tell one more lie about me, I'm going to tie a knot in your tail you'll never get out. I don't know what fantasy world you're living in, but I won't stand for it, do you hear me?"

I left them there arguing, wondering why Runion had come up with such a flimsy response to my question about Gretel's place. His account of what had happened stretched the boundaries of believability, and I wondered why that surprised me. The man reminded me of the old joke that said the only way you could tell when a lawyer was lying was to see if his lips were moving. I'd trust Gary Cragg first, and the attorney at River's Edge didn't have much credibility with me. If Runion was telling the truth, he hadn't approached Gretel first at all. The idea of a crank call just didn't resonate with me. But if Runion was after her shop, was it possible her store was part of a bigger purchase? I didn't know, but at least I knew one way I might be able to find out. I had a source inside City Hall who just might be able to help me separate fact from fiction.

I found Frannie Wilson locking up her office door at the Register of Deeds when I got to city hall.

"Harrison Black, I can't believe my eyes. You, of all people, out playing hooky."

Frannie was a big fan of candlemaking, and had been

one of Belle's first customers at the shop. She looked like somebody's grandmother, but had a sassy, playful streak that always caught me off guard.

"I haven't seen you lately, so I wanted to make sure all was well with the world."

Frannie said loud enough so everyone in the building could hear, "I know you didn't kill that woman, Harrison." In a lower voice, she added, "There, do you think that helped?"

"At this point it couldn't hurt."

"Things are as bad as all that, are they?" she asked, scowling. "I don't understand folks around here turning on you, Harrison. I know in my heart you never would have shot that woman."

"Thanks." I was grateful for her support, and wished she'd stopped there.

Not Frannie. "Now I can see you running her down with your truck, or even whacking her over the head with one of those monster candles you like so much, but shooting her? No sir, I don't buy it, not for a second."

"It's good to know you believe in me."

"So what brings you here? I don't wager for one minute that you missed my ugly mug."

"Frannie, you know you're one of my best-looking customers."

She cackled at that, then added, "Then you've got to do something to pretty up your clientele. Enough of this idle chitchat. Why are you here?"

"I need to know if Greg Runion's been up to anything in the downtown district lately; say, right around Gretel Barnett's shop."

She pretended to look shocked. "Harrison, you should know better than to ask me something like that." As she spoke, she nodded her head vigorously. "I could get in serious trouble giving out that kind of information." Then she winked, and added with a whisper, "It didn't turn out to be much, though, since he couldn't buy the whole block. There was one holdout, so the deal fell through for everyone. Guess who it was?"

"I don't have to guess. It was Gretel, wasn't it?"

Frannie nodded. "I don't have to tell you it didn't make her popular with the other folks wanting to sell to Runion. There are three people who own the rest of that block, and I'd be willing to believe that any one of them had a better reason to plug her than you did."

"You wouldn't mind telling me which three folks she crossed, would you?"

Frannie looked up and down the hallway, saw that it was empty, then said softly, "There's Martin Graybill, he owns The Ranch Restaurant. Then there's a man from Minnesota who's never set foot in North Carolina, as far as I can tell."

"Who's the third party?" I asked.

Frannie shook her head, then finally said, "If you tell a soul I told you, I'll deny it till I die, but you actually know the woman. The only other owner on that block is your star candlemaking student, Mrs. Henrietta Jorgenson herself."

Eight

"**MRS. J**? Are you sure?"

Frannie said, "Harrison, most of Micah's Ridge has no idea how much property that woman owns. She's the closest thing to a Rockefeller we have around here."

"If she's already wealthy, she wouldn't be too upset missing out on this deal, would she?" I couldn't believe Mrs. Jorgenson would hurt anyone because of money, when she already had so much of it already.

Frannie shook her head. "You don't know many rich folks, do you? There are two kinds I run across in my job, and they're as different as dogs and cats. There's one sort who are the best kind of folk around, and no one would ever know how much they've got by the way they act. Then there's the other kind, the ones that want every cent they can get their hands on, like it's some kind of race to the end. Do I need to tell you which type your Mrs. Jorgenson is? She's never given up a penny without making it squeal, except for her hobbies. In everything else, she's as shrewd and tight-fisted a woman as you'd ever want to run across."

"Thanks, Frannie, I appreciate the information. The next time you come in, your bill's on the house."

She said, "As much as I appreciate the offer, I'm not about to accept it, and you know it. I'll pay my own way, Harrison Black. I always have, and I always will."

As I headed back to At Wick's End, my mind was buzzing with ideas. I'd added two suspects in my hunt, one that didn't surprise me and one that had knocked me off balance. I had no trouble visualizing Runion as a killer, but I just couldn't see Mrs. Jorgenson doing it, despite what Frannie had told me. I wondered if Gretel's brother would be interested in completing the deal his sister had refused. I'd surely like to talk to the beneficiary—the only person with a real concrete reason to want Gretel dead—but if the police couldn't find him, I didn't have a prayer. It was time to head back to River's Edge.

I WORKED THE last hour with Eve, and though I could tell she was dying of curiosity to hear about what I'd been up to, I kept my thoughts to myself. I just couldn't bring myself to tell her about Mrs. Jorgenson's possible involvement in Gretel's death. I wasn't even willing to acknowledge it myself, let alone say the words aloud.

After we locked the door and ran our reports from the meager totals, she said, "Well, if there's nothing else, I'll be going."

"See you in the morning," I said.

She huffed once, then let herself out, not bothering to lock the door behind her. I waited a minute, then walked over and slid the deadbolt into place. I still had to make out the deposit, then head to the bank. I'd learned early on that the shop's business had to come first. If there was time and energy left over, I could spend it however I wished. I had to admit, At Wick's End—and River's Edge in general— was a great amount of work to handle. I found myself admiring my great-aunt Belle more every day as I tried to follow in her footsteps.

After I dropped off the deposit at the bank, I decided to head straight back to the complex instead of grabbing a bite out. There was peanut butter and jelly in my larder, and while it wasn't a meal fit for a king, it would do for me. I slapped a sandwich together, made a tall glass of chocolate milk, then headed up to the roof. It was a little brisk for a picnic, but I needed some open space around me, and there was no place in the world more open than my secret getaway.

Though it was still early, darkness had crept in like a thief and stolen the last bits of sunlight while I'd been making my meal. The roof was shrouded in shadows, but I knew the turf well enough to head unerringly to the cache holding my chair and blanket. As I settled in to eat, I marveled once again at the stars above me, punctuating the night with their brilliance. There was a halo around the moon, and a crisp bite to the air that made me feel alive. The wind kicked up off the river, and I shivered against its intrusion. It was a small price to pay for the sights and sounds I was experiencing. As I ate my sandwich, I took in my surroundings, happy that Belle had entrusted it all to me, but sad about the way I'd acquired it all.

The cold finally drove me back inside before I was ready to give up the sky. I promised myself that when summer came, I'd bring a hammock and stand up on the roof if I had to hoist it with a crane so I could spend a night high above Micah's Ridge.

As I rinsed my dishes back in my apartment, there was

a pounding on my door, and from the sound of it, whoever wanted me wasn't there to share good news.

I opened the door and found Markum standing in the hallway.

"You're back early," I said, stepping aside as the big man came into my apartment. "Did something go wrong?"

Markum had always been sketchy about what he did, and whenever I pressed him, he'd always say, "You'll have to come with me sometime before you'll get a word out of me," and he'd leave it at that. I kept promising myself that someday I'd join him on one of his adventures. Markum had offered the possibility of great reward, and an equal amount of risk.

He laughed heartily, and I knew that everything had turned out all right for him. "On the contrary, my friend, things went better than I had any right to expect. You should have been with me; the Florida Keys were beautiful. In fact, if you hadn't been in a spot of trouble back here, I might have hung around a few weeks as a reward."

"I hate that you came back on my account," I said.

He slapped my shoulder, and I felt it sting. "Harrison, there are always pretty sights and even prettier girls around the next corner, but not when a friend needs a hand."

"So what happened on your trip?" I asked, never expecting an answer.

He looked at me a few moments, then said, "I had to deal with some pirates."

"Come on, if you don't want to tell me, that's fine, but give me some credit."

Markum shook his head. "There are more pirates than the ones with eye patches and parrots, my friend."

"You mean like software pirating, that kind of thing?"

"No, I'm talking about pirates on the water. A friend of a friend I know from another life called me with a horrific story. Seems a pretty bad man and his friends found out a young woman named Sammie Jo was alone on her yacht, so they decided to move in and make themselves comfortable, even if Sammie Jo had different ideas altogether."

"Why didn't she call the police?" I asked.

Markum shrugged. "There were threats made, very real ones at that. These fellows had some rather alarming manners. Sammie Jo managed to make one telephone call before they found her cell phone. She called Lisa and Lisa called me."

"So what did you do?" I asked. I couldn't believe Markum was telling his story so calmly. My heart was racing just listening.

"Well, I had a nice long chat with the gentlemen in question, and they decided to vacate the premises and not come back."

"So you convinced them quicker than you thought you would?"

Markum shook his head. "I knew it wouldn't take long to set them straight, but finding them was my main problem. Turns out they were holed up on Big Pine Key, and they weren't trying to hide their presence there."

"How did you convince them?" I asked.

Markum laughed. "You're a curious fellow, aren't you? Let's just say that pirates aren't the only ones who can make somebody walk the plank. By the time they all made it to shore, I knew they wouldn't be bothering the lady in question again."

I tried to get more out of him, but he seemed to regret sharing what he had. I finally said, "Was Sammie Jo satisfied with the outcome?"

"She was satisfied enough to bank my next excursion to Alaska and become a silent partner."

"You haven't given up on that, have you?" Markum had

been thwarted attempting something in Alaska, and it was one of the few times he'd come back with his tail between his legs. I wondered about the kind of people who could do that to a man with so much positive energy and sheer force of will.

"I'm breathing, aren't I? You're still welcome to sign on and come with me."

"I'll take a rain check," I said. "I've got all I can handle here."

He ran a hand through that thick black hair of his. "Just wait. I'll talk you into coming yet."

"You'll have to do better than you've been able to do so far," I said.

Markum looked me up and down and said, "You're scared, aren't you?"

"You bet I am, and I'm not afraid to admit it."

Markum cackled with delight. "Then I want you on my team for sure. It's the fools who aren't afraid that end up getting hurt. Now what's going on with you?"

I brought him up to date, hesitated when it came to the part about Mrs. Jorgenson, but I went ahead and gave him the details of everything I'd found out. After all, what good was it to have a sounding board if I didn't come clean about everything I'd uncovered?

"You've been busy," he said. "I'm impressed."

"I feel like I'm spinning my wheels," I admitted. "I'm even more confused now than I was before."

"Harrison, you're going about it the right way. If you're not ready to come to any conclusions yet, it just means that you haven't gathered enough information. Now let's sit down and think this through. Where do we attack next?"

"I don't know," I admitted. "I've been trying to track down Gretel's brother, but I can't figure out how to do that if the police can't even find him."

"How do you know they're even looking? Come over to my office, I've got an idea or two about that."

I locked up my apartment and walked down the hallway to Markum's office with him. I traced a finger across the gold leaf letters SALVAGE AND RECOVERY on his door as I passed through it.

He'd changed some of the travel posters on the walls since I'd been inside, and I was staring at one of Belize as he slipped behind his desk. Markum pulled a notebook computer out and started tapping some keys.

I asked, "What are you doing, looking for him on Google?"

"I've got a better search engine than that, my friend. At least I do for the information we're looking for."

"Do I want to know more than that?" I asked.

Markum laughed. "Probably not. Hum," he said as he stared at his screen. "Now isn't that interesting?"

"What is?"

"There's no photograph of Hans Barnett on file here, though there are several of Gretel Barnett."

"So he's camera shy," I said. "I know lots of folks that don't like to have their pictures taken."

Markum scratched his head. "But do they hate it enough to move to a state with no photos on their driver's licenses?"

"That could just be a coincidence," I said.

Markum shrugged. "Maybe, but it appears our boy has been avoiding the camera for years. Wait a second, let me try something else." He tapped more keys, then said, "Blast it all, that's a dead end, too."

"Do we really need a picture of the man to track him down?" I asked.

"It wouldn't hurt. Besides, I find it helps me in my search if I can match a face with every name. It can be embarrassing to bump into your quarry and let him slip right past you just because you weren't thorough enough to find out what the gent looked like. I've got other sources, but not at my fingertips. Let me try something else." After a few moments, he smiled gently. "That's more like it. Here's a web page Gretel did herself a few years ago. It hasn't been updated for ages, but there's something about her brother here." As Markum read, he shared the information with me. "Okay, based on what she's written here, the gentleman in question has gray hair that was once brown, he's of average height and weight, he's got cool blue eyes—whatever that means—he's left-handed and he used to collect rare coins. His résumé is a human resources director's nightmare. From this one entry, it looks like he's worked in a bank, on a farm, and at a hardware store; he's worked as a carnie on the midway and he's been a masseur. It's not much to go on, is it?"

"It's more than I was able to track down. You got all that from her web page?" I was impressed. While I knew a few things about computers, mostly my skills covered just enough to be able to sell them in another life before I'd come to At Wick's End. I'd even resisted getting a cell phone, mainly because I didn't want to be that accessible to anyone.

"Some people treat these pages like diaries," Markum said. "It's amazing what you can find if you just know where to look."

I thought about it for a moment, then said, "Do you think it's possible that Hans had something to do with his sister's death?"

Markum tapped a few keys, then logged off. He said, "A good rule of thumb when somebody is murdered is to look around for motive. Everything else usually falls into place after you've determined the reason why; there's got to be somebody out there looking to gain something, and I don't just mean money. Hans Barnett is the obvious choice, but since he doesn't appear to be anywhere around, we need to cast our nets a little farther."

"I still don't think Mrs. Jorgenson had anything to do with what happened."

"And that's based on what, your growing friendship with the woman? Harrison, that's one of the things I admire about you, but just because you like someone doesn't meant they're incapable of some pretty terrible things."

I hoped he wasn't talking about himself, but I was learning not to press him if I wasn't sure I was going to like the answer.

He leaned back in his chair, then said, "You haven't said much about Pearly."

"He couldn't have had anything to do with this," I said. I may have had some doubt in my mind, but I would defend him with my last breath.

Markum scowled. "If it's not profit behind the trouble, it could be love."

"Do you honestly think Pearly could have had anything to do with Gretel's murder? Come on, Markum, we're talking about our friend here."

Markum picked up a pen from the desktop and began rolling it between his hands. "I admit it. I've grown to like the man myself, but whose word do we have but his own that he's the one who broke it off with Gretel? Maybe it was the other way around. You spotted him at the fair on the morning of the murder, we can't forget that. I'll grant you that Pearly doesn't appear to be the type to do something like this, but love can make you do strange things, my friend."

I shook my head. "Not this. I'm not sure I'd believe it if Pearly told me himself."

Markum shrugged. "So I'll keep my doubts to myself

about our handyman from now on unless I find something a little more substantial than what we've got so far. Is that a deal?"

"I guess so," I said. I didn't like the fact that Pearly was suspect in any way, but until I could prove his innocence to Markum—and to myself—I'd have to do my best to find the truth. Markum deserved all the facts if I was going to ask him to help me.

He ticked off his fingers as he spoke. "So we've got brother Hans, Pearly, Mrs. Jorgenson, Runion the developer, Martin Graybill and the Minnesota Mystery Man so far. Have I left anyone else out? Who else's life has Gretel's touched?"

"You mean besides me?" I asked.

Markum laughed. "For the purposes of this exercise, we're exempting you, Harrison."

"I appreciate that," I said, "Her cousin Jubal has been working with her at the candleshop, but from what he told me, he doesn't inherit a thing. He's just sticking around until Hans shows up."

"You know, maybe we should have a talk with Gretel's lawyer. I wonder if we're jumping to the wrong conclusion here."

"What do you mean?"

Markum said, "We all are under the impression that Gretel left everything to her brother, but do we know that for a fact? Who's this attorney happen to be? I just hope it's not Cragg, though it would make things easier."

"Come on," I said, "Just because I have a key to his place doesn't mean I'm going to snoop around in his office."

"Now who said anything about you doing something like that? I was just thinking out loud."

"Jubal told me the attorney Gretel hired was ancient,

but that's all I remember. If he told me the man's name, it's slipped my mind."

Markum said, "Then you'll have to speak with Jubal tomorrow and get that memory refreshed."

"I'm not going to help you break in to somebody's office, Markum."

"Harrison, I'm shocked, absolutely shocked, by your implication."

I started to say something, but the mock severity of his gaze made me laugh instead. "Sorry, I didn't mean to impugn your honor," I said.

"I'll forgive you this time," he said, the gleam in his eye brightening. "So it's settled. Tomorrow you speak with Jubal and get me that name, then I'll take it from there." Markum's phone rang before I could protest further, and after a moment's consultation with his caller, he put a hand over the receiver and said, "It's Sammie Jo from the Keys."

"The pirates aren't back, are they?"

Markum smiled softly. "Not with the lesson I gave them. No, it sounds like she misses me."

"You'd better watch out, Markum, she may be getting too attached to you."

"You worry about your problems and I'll worry about mine," he said with a smile. "We'll talk again tomorrow."

I left Markum to his telephone call, a small part of me jealous that there was someone in the world who missed him. I wasn't seeing anyone at the moment. In fact, I barely dated, and I missed that last phone call before bed, someone to wrap up the day with. I wished Sammie Jo luck in settling Markum down as I got ready for bed, but knew she'd have an epic task before her.

Markum was not the settling kind.

In all honesty, I was beginning to wonder if I was the

type myself. No, I was just going through a dry spell when it came to my love life. I missed having a steady relationship with a woman, and hoped to have one again sometime in the future. For the moment, though, I had a very demanding mistress in River's Edge, and I doubted she'd take kindly to any distractions from my attention to her.

Nine

I was startled the next morning when Mrs. Jorgenson—my erstwhile star student and newest suspect—walked into the candleshop.

"Harrison, we need to talk."

That tone of voice couldn't lead to anything good. Trying to cajole her out of her dark mood, I asked, "Are you ready for your next lesson? I could probably squeeze you in now before things get busy." In all honesty, I didn't have very high hopes that business would pick up any more than the trickle of customers we'd had the past few days.

She shook her head. "No, I don't have time for that right now. There is something we need to resolve."

"Why don't we go back to my office then." I followed her through the candleshop, but instead of the usual browsing she did every time she'd visited At Wick's End, her gaze was focused straight ahead of us.

I settled into my chair and said, "I wasn't sure we'd see you again."

She scoffed. "Harrison Black, I'm not about to be driven off because of rumors and whispered accusations."

"Funny, but I was beginning to suspect that was exactly what happened."

Her back stiffened. "Young man, are you intentionally baiting me?"

I knew it was time to back off. Not only did I need Mrs. Jorgenson's income from her lessons and purchases, but I also wanted her close enough to question. Like it or not, she was one of my suspects, and alienating her wouldn't do me a bit of good. I took a deep breath, then said, "I'm sorry. I've been under a great amount of strain lately. I didn't mean to take it out on you."

Her hard expression softened. "I know it's been difficult for you. I'm willing to give you some latitude, but don't push me too hard."

"Understood. I heard you're under some pressure of your own."

That certainly got her attention. "What exactly do you mean by that?"

"Runion told me he was buying up Gretel Barnett's block, and I happened to hear that you own property close to Flickering Lights." I watched her expression, but if there was any change there, it was too subtle for me to see.

"Mr. Runion spoke out of place."

"So it's not true?"

Mrs. Jorgenson snapped, "It's irrelevant. Harrison, I own a great many properties around Micah's Ridge and beyond. That pipe dream of his wouldn't have affected me much one way or the other." She was a bright woman, and it didn't take long for my question to click. "Are you accusing me of anything?" she asked with deadly calm.

"No, Ma'am. I was just hoping you might know something about what happened to Gretel."

My backpedaling helped some, but not nearly enough. "I don't make it a habit of getting involved in murder, no matter what your own predilection appears to be. Now if you'll excuse me, I don't have time for this nonsense."

"Listen, I'm sorry if I was out of line. I just hate being a suspect in murder."

"I can appreciate your point of view, but pardon me if I'm not all that eager to take your place. Good day."

I couldn't stop her from storming out, nor was I certain I wanted to try. Was her righteous indignation real, or was she upset that I was on her trail? Either way, I realized with a sinking feeling that I may have just driven off my one guaranteed source of income. But the alternative could be going to prison for a crime I didn't commit. I had to explore every possible trail that could lead me to the truth, no matter what the consequences.

As I came out of the office, Eve said, "Harrison, do you have a death wish? I've never seen anyone as furious as she was when she stormed out of here."

"I may have crossed the line," I admitted.

"Well, don't just stand there. Go apologize."

"I didn't say I was wrong. All I'm willing to admit is that I may have pushed her a little hard."

Eve gestured around the shop. "So you pick this moment to alienate our best customer. Brilliant."

I thought about it a moment or two, then realized Eve was right. I shouldn't have pressed Mrs. Jorgenson, certainly not without more information than I had. I hurried to the parking lot to see if I could catch her, but by the time I got outside, she was already gone. It appeared that I'd blown my last chance with my star student and benefactor.

To my surprise, we had a relatively busy day at the candleshop, though I was too morose to enjoy it. I knew Markum was expecting me to get Gretel's lawyer's name from Jubal, but I didn't have time to slip away. I was thankful for the shoppers and didn't want to leave a buzzing store. Maybe things were finally easing up. I was happy *The Gunpowder Gazette* hadn't printed any more photos or stories linking me to Gretel's murder. At least on that front, things were improving.

By the end of the day, I actually had enough income to justify taking it to the bank for more of a reason than just routine. As I filled out the slip and prepared the deposit, Eve took one of our Shaker-style baskets we were starting to carry made by a local craftsman and began filling it with candles and accessories.

After she was finished, she plopped the basket down in front of me.

"What's this for?" I asked.

"It's your apology to Mrs. Jorgenson."

I pushed the basket away. "What makes you think she'd even see me?"

"What makes you think she won't?"

"You're kidding, right? I've got a feeling the way she stormed out of here was a pretty good indication that she might not be all that eager to greet me."

"Thus the goodwill basket," Eve said. "Harrison, the longer you let this go, the more permanent the rift might become. Make amends before she convinces herself she doesn't need us anymore."

I took the deposit and started for the door. "I think we've already crossed that particular line."

"You owe it the candleshop to at least try," Eve said firmly, collecting the basket, then pressing it into my hands. "Swallow your pride, Harrison."

I took the offering from her, albeit reluctantly. "I don't even know where she lives."

Eve said, "She's in Parsons Ferry. Here, I wrote her address down for you."

I took it and stuffed the note into my pocket. "Okay, I'll do it. You realize she's probably going to slam the door in my face."

"From the way she looked when she left, you've got it coming, wouldn't you say?"

I drove to the bank and made the deposit, though it would have been much closer going to Mrs. Jorgenson's first. Every plea I could think of was rejected as quickly as I thought of it. What could I say, that I was sorry? Was I, though? The more I thought about it, the more I had to acknowledge to myself that I was. I'd let my imagination get the best of me. I didn't care what Markum thought. There was no way Mrs. Jorgenson would shoot Gretel. She might try to run her out of business and Micah's Ridge, but murder? No, I just couldn't see it. I'd let the fact that I was under police suspicion cloud my judgment about a friend, and I vowed to never let that happen again.

Parsons Ferry was the ritziest development in Micah's Ridge. I hadn't been there since I'd moved into town, but I'd heard enough around that should have prepared me for what I found. The houses—perched on the edge of the Gunpowder River—were extraordinary: mansions on the water. I hadn't even slowed at the guarded gate, just tossing a wave to the man inside. The builder had tried to make the development an exclusive one, and the imposing guard's station was just one of the many ways it tried to discourage casual visitors. But an article in *The Gunpowder Gazette* a few months earlier had disclosed that since the state of North Carolina maintained the roads, there was no way access could be limited legally. Cruising the neighborhood had become a new hobby for some of Micah's Ridge's less wealthy citizens, and I'd heard complaints from some of my customers that something was going to have to be done to curb it.

The Jorgenson property was surrounded by a high stucco wall, taking up three expensive lots facing the river side by side by side. The imposing structure greeted me as I drove up, and I felt more than a little conspicuous in my Ford truck. At least I'd had sense enough not to show up in my battered old Dodge. Still, I felt like I was wearing bibbed overalls to the prom as I parked in front of Mrs. Jorgenson's house.

I couldn't believe it when an actual butler answered the door just as I rang the bell. He studied me with a glance and blocked my way before I could step a foot inside.

"Yes?" he said in a voice that hinted of a British accent.

"I'm here to see Mrs. Jorgenson," I said, holding the basket of goodies in front of me like a shield.

"I'm sorry, sir, but she's unavailable at the moment." Not much of an apology, no offer to check with her first, just a flat and final refusal.

"Listen, tell her I need to speak with her. My name's Harrison Black. I run At Wick's End."

"I'm afraid her instructions were most specific," he said.

This was getting me nowhere. It was obvious I wasn't going to be able to brush past her guardian.

"Fine. Give this to her and tell her I'm sorry," I said as I thrust the basket into his hands. He accepted the offering with gentle distaste, then shut the door on me before I had a chance to say another word.

I got back into the truck and was just starting to drive away when he suddenly reappeared, waving me down. I rolled down the window, and he said, "Please take this back, sir. Mrs. Jorgenson isn't interested in your gift."

"Tough," I said. "I won't take it. Tell her I'm just as

stubborn as she is. I can't make her accept my apology, but I'll be dipped in candlewax if she thinks I'm going to let her insult me by refusing my gift."

I drove off, half-expecting the man to throw the basket into the back of my truck. When I glanced back in my rearview mirror, I saw him shaking his head and staring at the basket as if it were diseased.

I'd done all I could. If Mrs. Jorgenson declined my offering and my apology, there was nothing else I could do about it. I refused to beat myself up about it anymore. It was time to move on, forget about my star student and get back to running my candleshop.

At least I wouldn't have to face Eve until morning. I had some free time on my hands, and I suddenly had no desire to go back to River's Edge. I was finding that with the lessening of daylight hours in the winter, I was spending more and more time in the evening burrowing into my apartment, and though I enjoyed my time alone, it was getting to be a habit I was going to have to break.

Though my checking account was anemic, I decided to treat myself to a pizza and some of April May's company at A Slice of Heaven.

The place was crowded, and I worried about finding a table, when Heather Bane from River's Edge called out to me, "Harrison. Over here."

She'd been the one to introduce me to April and her pizzeria, and I joined her gratefully. I noticed that Heather was dressed much nicer than was normal for her, and I said, "Are you here by yourself?"

Heather nodded. "I had a date, actually, but it appears that he stood me up."

"What a jerk," I said.

"I don't really mind, to be honest with you. My girlfriend's cousin set it up, and I was dreading the whole ordeal."

"Then we'll drink a toast to the dumb cluck and have fun in spite of him."

April made her way through the crowd and studied me before speaking. "Please tell me you're not him."

"I'm not him," I said simply.

April smiled. "That's a relief. Heather, are you going to let this riffraff sit at your table, or should I put him back in the kitchen?"

She pretended to consider the offer, then said, "He might as well stay. That way I won't look like a pig when I eat an entire pizza by myself. Bring us a medium special, unless you want to join us."

April looked tempted, then studied the room. "I'd better not. Things are hopping tonight. One special, coming up."

She started to leave, then said, "Harrison, have you picked your song yet?"

"I'm still thinking about it. How long do I have?" April had a policy that with every ten pizzas purchased, the customer could pick one song for her jukebox. The only restrictions were that it had to be from the fifties or sixties, and if the customer didn't renew it with another ten pizzas in two months, it was pulled from the rotation.

April said, "I'll give you a few more days. Do you want to look at the catalog again?"

"No, I've got it down to two choices."

She said, "Care to enlighten me?"

"Now what fun would that be?" I said.

She swatted at me with a bar towel, then said, "I'll send your beer over in a minute."

After she was gone, Heather said, "So how are things, Harrison?"

"We're actually starting to get some of our customers back, if you can believe it."

"That's wonderful news," Heather said. "Has Morton finally decided to believe you?" Heather wasn't our sheriff's biggest fan, and while I didn't agree with her low opinion of him, I knew she had reasons of her own.

"He's still not sure, but at least he's looking at other folks, too."

"Enough about that," Heather said. "Let's talk about something not related to murder. I've been meaning to ask you, where's Pearly off to? Don't tell me he actually broke down and took a vacation."

"He had to get away. Pearly's pretty torn up about what happened. Did you know he'd been dating Gretel on the sly?"

Heather shook her head. "I thought that was just a casual thing."

"Apparently it was more than that. It gets worse. They broke it off the night before she died."

Heather said, "Poor Pearly. I can't imagine how bad he must be feeling."

"I know. I told him to take some time off, but I was still surprised when he took me up on it." I noticed a familiar face as Erin Talbot walked in, and I waved to her.

"Do you mind if she joins us," I asked. I was eager to find out how her rafting trip had gone.

"Not at all," Heather said, a touch of frost in her voice.

"That's okay, we don't have to invite her."

Heather said curtly, "Don't be silly. There's plenty of room for her."

I shrugged, beckoned her toward us, and Erin walked over. Her face was sunburned from the trip, and her hair looked a shade lighter than it had the last time I'd seen her.

"Hi, guys," Erin said as she stood beside our table. She

noticed Heather's dress and added, "Sorry, I don't want to interrupt anything."

"Don't worry, this isn't a date," Heather said. "At least not for Harrison."

"Some joker stood her up," I explained.

Heather said, "Gee, thanks for spreading the news, Harrison. I was afraid there might be somebody in Micah's Ridge who didn't know about my disastrous love life."

Erin said, "I won't say a word, if that's what you're worried about."

Heather said, "Oh, I didn't mean anything by it. I'm just touchy, I guess."

"You have every reason to be, if you ask me. Men can be so thoughtless sometimes."

"Believe me, you're preaching to the choir," Heather said.

"Hey, I'm still here," I said. "Remember?"

"So you're taking up for this cretin?" Erin asked coolly.

"Me? You've got to be kidding. I'm one of the good guys, remember?"

Erin said, "That's better." She looked over at the bar as two men left their stools. "It was nice seeing you two. I need to go grab one of those spots."

"Nonsense, you can join us," Heather said.

"Are you sure? I don't mean to butt in."

"I'm positive. Harrison, are you going to scoot over and make room?"

"I'm scooting," I said as Erin sat beside me.

April showed up with my beer, then did a double take when she saw Erin sitting with us. "Now I know you're not him."

"Thank goodness for that," Erin said. "And thank you for noticing."

"Not much gets past me," April said. "What can I get you?"

"I'll have one of those," she said, pointing to my beer, "and bring me a meatball sub when their food gets here."

"I'm on it," she said.

"So how was the rafting trip?" I asked after April left.

"It was amazing. We saw some incredible wildlife, and the rapids were really wild after all the rain they've been having. To be honest with you, we thought about canceling the trip, but I'm glad we went ahead. One run usually takes seven hours. We did it in less than four. You really should go with us next time." She turned to Heather and said, "You, too. It's great fun."

Heather shivered. "No thanks. The closest I ever want to get to a river again is having lunch on the steps in front of River's Edge. I nearly drowned when I turned my canoe over last year, and the thought of going out on the water again terrifies me."

"I didn't know that," I said. "I love my kayak."

She smiled. "I know. You really fly up and down the river in front of the complex." I looked over Heather's shoulder and saw Sheriff Morton come in. Heather and Erin followed my gaze as he spotted us and headed our way.

"Now what does he want?" Heather asked.

"We'll know in a second," I said, hoping that the sheriff wasn't bringing me any more bad news.

Morton nodded his head toward my dining companions, then said, "Harrison, I need a word with you."

"Whatever you have to say, you can tell me in front of them," I said.

"Okay, have it your way. When's the last time you saw that handyman of yours?"

"He's on vacation," I said.

Morton frowned. "That's too bad. I really need to talk to him."

"What about?" I asked.

"I'm sure if you use your imagination, you can guess," Morton said.

"Surely you don't think he had anything to do with Gretel's murder, do you?"

The sheriff shrugged. "That's what I need to talk to him about. I thought you'd be happy I was looking at someone else."

Before I could say anything, Heather interrupted. "You should be looking for the real killer."

"That's what I'm trying to do." It was obvious neither one of them was fond of the other. He turned back to me and said, "So where did he go, Harrison?"

"All I know is that he's somewhere in the mountains."

"Do you happen to know when he's coming back? If he's coming back?" Before Heather could say anything, he held up a hand. "Save it, Heather. Have Pearly call me when he gets in town, Harrison. If you hear from him, tell him to get back here as soon as humanly possible, you got that?"

I promised, and the sheriff left. After he was gone, Erin asked plaintively, "Would someone please tell me what's going on?"

I brought her up to speed on recent events with interjections from Heather.

After we'd finished, Erin said, "And the sheriff's actually been treating you like a suspect? Harrison, that's awful."

"It hasn't been pretty, but I'm no happier about him going after Pearly now." I hadn't shared any of the inside information I had about the handyman, not wanting to add any more speculation to the mix.

Our food arrived a short time later, but the joy of it was lost on me.

Armstrong had indeed shifted his focus, just as I'd been hoping.

Unfortunately, it appeared that it now lay squarely on my handyman and good friend's broad shoulders.

Ten

COME down to my office, no matter what time you get in. The note on my apartment door was from Markum, and I realized he'd be expecting the name of Gretel's lawyer. I didn't want to tell him I'd been too busy working at the candleshop, but I didn't have any choice. I didn't even bother going inside my own place first. I just pulled the note off and walked down the hallway.

His door was standing wide open, something I'd seen only twice since I'd taken over River's Edge.

I knocked on the frame, then stuck my head inside. "What's up?"

He looked up from a map he was studying and said, "I kind of miss the old Soviet Union. At least then I knew where everything was."

"Is that map for business or pleasure?" I asked.

He said, "Believe me, I wouldn't plan a vacation to Eastern Europe. I've got a lead that might be too good to pass up, though. Want to come with me? Eve can watch the candleshop, and Pearly can take care of River's Edge while we're gone."

"If he's not in jail," I said.

"What's going on?" Markum asked as he pushed the map away.

"Morton came by A Slice of Heaven tonight looking for Pearly. He found out our handyman was dating Gretel, and that they ended it rather harshly the night before she was murdered."

Markum said, "He can't do anything with that, unless he knows that Pearly was in New Conover when it happened."

"Yeah, well, I'm guessing he found out. Morton acted like Pearly was fleeing the country when I told him he'd gone to the mountains."

Markum said, "Can you blame him? What ties does Pearly have to the community? This place is the only family he's got around here."

I hadn't known that about Pearly. "Are you saying you think that he might have run away? I don't believe it."

Markum snorted once, then said, "Neither do I. But I have to give Morton some slack. It doesn't look good."

While Markum was still frowning, I said, "I didn't have a chance to talk to Jubal today, so I'm still not sure who Gretel's attorney was."

Markum smiled. "The man's name is Cyrus Blain. He's got an office in Hickory, but he spends most of his time around here."

"Now how did you find that out?"

"You're not the only one with resources in town. I went to see him this afternoon. It was quite illuminating."

"He told you something about the will?"

Markum put his feet up on his desk. "It wasn't exactly a free exchange of information, but I managed to pick up a thing or two. The man runs a satellite operation here in town. His office looks like two broom closets stuck together. He doesn't even have a secretary, and his files are in the waiting area. The old buzzard kept me waiting twenty minutes, and by the time he showed me into his office, I'd found what I was looking for. Take a peek at these."

He took his feet off the desk, retrieved a folder from the bottom drawer and slid it across the desk to me. Inside, there were half a dozen black-and-white photographs, each showing a different page of a legal document.

"You had the guts to stand there and take pictures? Why didn't you just ask him if you could use the copier?"

Markum grinned. "I would have, but it's in the office he's in, and I thought that might be pushing it."

"But taking pictures of the will wasn't?" I asked, marveling at the clarity of the shots.

Markum smiled, then pulled a pen from his pocket. "This comes in handy sometimes when I need to document what I'm doing." He handed me the pen and I saw that it hadn't been designed to write at all. Instead, it appeared to be a tiny camera. Markum explained, "I got it off the Internet. I wasn't sure it would be worthwhile having, but I've been surprised. Never mind the gadget; look at the papers."

I studied the photographed documents for a few minutes, then said, "It's what Jubal told me. Gretel's brother Hans gets everything. There are a few minor bequests, but nothing that amounts to much."

"Think again. Did you see that Pearly was mentioned?"

"Yeah, that surprised me. It took me a second to remember that Pearly's given name is Parsons. I wonder if he's related to the people Parsons Landing is named after?"

"Let's not worry about his genealogy right now. What do you think about him being mentioned in the will?"

"You know, they hadn't been dating all that long. I can't imagine her leaving him anything. It's not much, though. How much could a pair of antique ceremonial masks be worth, anyway?"

"Don't kid yourself. I did a little research while I was waiting for you to show up. Look at this." He hit a few keys on his laptop, then pivoted the screen around so I could see it. There was a pair of dark wooden masks on display, with a paragraph on their importance. "So? I still don't see a price."

"First look at who the masks belong to."

I scanned down and saw that Gretel Barnett was the registered owner. "How'd you find this?"

"I did a little research, Harrison. This is an auction house I've used in the past. It's a place where provenance is not all that important, if you know what I mean. Scan a little more."

I scrolled down and saw the opening bid on the masks. "Forty grand? You've got to be kidding me."

Markum attached a cable from his computer to a printer tucked under his desk, made a copy, then handed the listing to me. As I studied it, he said, "It appears Pearly and Gretel were a lot closer than we figured. I can't imagine her making that kind of bequest on a whim."

"And with their breakup, there's no doubt Gretel was going to change this will pretty quickly. It certainly looks bad for Pearly."

I picked up the will again and asked, "Was she nuts? She leaves something worth this much to Pearly, but then there's her cousin Jubal—a man she likes enough to have him help run her shop—and he's not even mentioned. I don't get it."

"I imagine that might be why Morton's so eager to speak with Pearly. I wouldn't mind having a word or two with him myself."

I tapped another page of the document and asked, "Why am I surprised she had this much money and property? I was under the impression she put everything she owned into her candleshop."

Markum said, "It's not all that unusual for folks with lots of money to hide its existence. If she'd been determined to follow through on her threat of burying you, she could have given candles away for the next forty years and never felt the pinch."

"I guess you're right. I wonder if Jubal knows how much his cousin was worth?"

Markum said, "I highly doubt it. Harrison, I once knew a husband and wife who were each independently wealthy in their own right. They both ended up hiring me to find out what the other was worth after a mutual friend bragged about something I'd done for him."

"Did you?" I asked.

"No, that's not really my line of work. I did recommend the same accountant to each of them. Those two didn't have much imagination. They both hired him."

"So you didn't get a dime from it?"

He laughed. "Don't kid yourself. The finder's fee I got for sending them to James was enough to pay for a month in Bali."

"Pearly can do a lot more than that with the proceeds from the sale of those masks. I'm sure in the sheriff's mind it's enough of a motive for murder."

"No doubt that's why he's looking for our friend. The only question is, what do we do about it?"

I stifled a yawn, then said, "I'm not really sure, and I'm too tired to think about it right now. It's been a long day."

Markum stood. "This probably could have waited until morning, but I wanted you to know."

I joined him as he walked to the door. "I appreciate you digging into this," I said. "You're a lot better at it than I am."

Markum locked his door behind us and said, "Don't sell yourself short, Harrison; you're getting better by the minute. Tell you what. Let me see what else I can come up with and we'll talk again soon."

"What about your plans in Eastern Europe?"

Markum said, "The project's not going anywhere, and I'm not about to jump into anything before I've had the chance to check it out a lot more than I have. We'll talk tomorrow."

After Markum was gone, I walked into the apartment, happy that the long day was nearly over.

I hadn't been getting many calls since the first deluge had stopped, and I'd become pretty lax when it came to checking my messages. I was surprised to see a flashing "2" on the machine.

I hit replay and heard Becka's voice. Her words came out in staccato. "Harrison. Pick up! He's here. I don't know what to do."

The connection broke, and as I listened to the second message, I started dialing Becka's number. Since I wasn't in the market for aluminum siding, I hit the pause button on the machine and waited for Becka to pick up.

Her line was busy.

I waited a few minutes, paced around the apartment, then tried her again.

Her line was still busy. All kinds of thoughts were swirling through my head. Had the stranger become bolder in his stalking? Was Becka trapped there, or worse yet, had something more ominous happened to her? Becka had a cell phone, but I didn't know the number anymore.

I tried her home number again. It was still busy. Or the line had been cut.

This was getting ridiculous. I hung up and dialed the operator. When I explained that it was an emergency, she tried the number, then came back on the line. "I'm afraid no one's there, sir."

I slammed the phone down and grabbed my keys as I ran out of the apartment. I just hoped I wasn't too late.

I GOT TO Becka's place in record time. She lived in Sky View, a complex that offered perks for young singles with disposable income, a place I'd never been able to afford. Becka lived in a corner unit on the bottom floor, and as I banged on the door, I noticed her car was sitting in its parking spot. She didn't answer my pounding, but a man next door came outside. He was in his mid-twenties, his blond hair pulled back in a ponytail, and his outfit carefully tailored.

"Come on, man, hold it down. I'm trying to chill over here."

"Have you seen Becka Lane tonight?"

He said, "I haven't even hit the bars yet. Is she yours?"

What a pig. "She's your neighbor. Are you saying you haven't met her yet? Did you just move in?"

"No, I've been here three months. She's kind of old for me, you know? More like your speed."

I let the obvious implied insult slip off me. I didn't have time to debate an unarmed opponent. "Where's the super live?"

"Vince? We call him our facilitator."

"I don't care if you call him princess, where does he live?"

"Chill, he's over in 27B."

I left without a word, hoping that Vince was not a twin to the man I'd been talking to. Becka's neighbor was a type I'd run into before, the carefully packaged but hopelessly shallow bachelor constantly on the prowl for the next morsel, never caring if the gift was all glamorous wrapping with nothing of merit inside. There were female counterparts as well, but I'd managed to avoid them over the years, or more likely, they'd avoided me. I'd never had the look they were interested in, driving a pickup instead of a convertible, wearing jeans and not Armani.

An older man with cropped gray hair and thick glasses answered on the first knock. "Can I help you?"

"I hope so. Are you Vince? I'm a friend of Becka Lane's. I got a disturbing telephone call from her tonight on my answering machine. When I tried to call her back, the line was busy, so I called the operator. No luck, it's off the hook. I need to get inside her apartment to check on her."

Vince stepped up close to me and said fiercely, "You think that's going to work on me? I wasn't born yesterday, jerk. Now get out of here before I break you in half."

I put my hands forward and said, "Hang on a second."

"Don't lie to me, you're the one who's been stalking her. If you don't leave Becka alone, I'll make you wish you had."

"I'm not the guy who's been following her. My name's Harrison Black. Becka and I used to date."

He studied me a second, then said, "If you two are so close, what's her mother's first name?"

"You've got to be kidding. I don't have a clue."

He started toward me again as I added, "I never called her anything but Mrs. Hurst."

That stopped him. "How'd you know her last name?"

"Why shouldn't I? We had dinner together a few times. It was a few times too many for me, if you want to know the truth."

Vince finally eased up his stance. "Yeah, I met her last month. She's a real charmer, isn't she? Wait right here and I'll grab my keys."

As we hurried back to Becka's apartment, I asked, "How well do you know her?"

"Becka and I have been friends since I took this job four months ago. Hey, are you the fella with the candleshop?"

"Guilty," I said.

"Yeah, it figures. I've been trying to figure out why she called you instead of me. No offense, but I'm a lot closer. What did she say?"

"She said the guy who's been stalking her was here."

Vince punched one hand with the other. "I'm going to kill him when I get my hands on him."

"Let's hope he's nowhere in sight," I said.

As we got to Becka's door, I expected Vince to charge in, but instead he rang her doorbell first, then knocked.

"Come on, we're wasting time. Let's go," I said.

"Sorry, I have to do it this way or I'll get fired." We waited ten seconds, then he said, "That's long enough."

As Vince approached the door with his key extended, to my surprise, it opened on its own.

Becka looked confused when she saw us both standing there. She was in a bathrobe and her hair was up in a towel. "I was in the shower," she said. "What are you two doing here?"

"I got your message, but when I tried to call you back,

your phone was off the hook. I've been worried sick about you."

She said, "If I don't hang the telephone up just right, it doesn't disconnect." Becka turned to Vince and said, "Sorry about that."

"Becka, you were supposed to call me if you saw that bum again."

She said, "I'm sorry, I know I should have. Harrison, when you weren't there, I started thinking maybe I was just jumping at shadows. It might not have been him after all."

"Yeah, well, next time call me, no matter what," Vince said. "I can be over here in thirty seconds, and I'll bring my baseball bat with me."

"Thanks, Vince," she said. The dismissal in her voice was obvious, and I turned to leave with him.

"Becka, I'm glad you're all right," I said.

"Harrison, why don't you come in for a minute?"

"Honestly, I'd like to, but it's late and I've got an early morning."

Vince said, "I could stick around if you want some company. You know, just to make sure everything's okay here."

Becka stifled a yawn, then said, "On second thought, I'd better take a rain check on company. I've got to get up early tomorrow myself. Sorry to bother you both."

Vince and I walked out in front of the apartment and stood there for a second in the glow from the security light. He finally asked, "You think she's going to be all right?"

It was obvious he was worried about her, too. "Yeah, at least for now. It's good of you to keep an eye on her."

"Hey, she's nice, you know? Not like some of the flakes we have around here. See you, Harrison. It was nice meeting you."

"Nice meeting you, too," I said.

As I drove back to River's Edge, I found myself wondering why Becka had called me instead of Vince. He was a lot closer than I was. It made sense enough when she'd rushed into the candleshop for protection, but I was a good ten minutes away from her apartment. I'd never been anyone's protector before, and I wasn't sure I liked the responsibility. Still, if she needed me, I'd be there, and what's more, Becka knew it.

I just hoped the next time she had a real emergency, I'd be able to get there in time.

Eleven

"I'D like to see the owner," I said the next morning as the hostess of The Ranch Restaurant approached me. She wore a fringed black vest and tall boots that nearly reached the hem of her skirt. I had decided the night before to pay a visit to Martin Graybill, one of the other property owners who'd hoped to make a deal with Runion. I wasn't scheduled to come into the candleshop till noon, though no one would probably have noticed if I took a few days off. While business was beginning to pick up a little again, it was still quite a bit off from what we'd been having before Gretel's murder.

"Is there something I can help you with?" the pretty redhead said.

"Sorry, I need to see Mr. Graybill."

"He won't be in for another half-hour. Would you like a table in the meantime?"

"No thanks, I'll just wait at the counter."

I found a seat on one of the spinning stools and looked

around. True to its name, The Ranch Restaurant sported all
kinds of cowboy memorabilia, including lassos hung over
the bar and a white counter dotted with cow spots. There
was country music playing in the background, and I half-
expected the waitresses to be wearing cowboy hats. They
did all sport similar fringed vests and shiny boots, just like
the hostess wore. I wondered what the waiters wore, but
when I scanned the workers, the only men I saw were
working back behind the grill. There was a signed photograph on the wall in front of me, and I wondered who
would want the autograph of a rodeo clown.

An older blonde with a big smile filled up my coffee
cup before I could refuse. "What can I get you?"

"This is fine," I said.

"Just coffee? Okay then. If you want something else, let
me know." She moved on down the line and refilled a few
more cups, each time pausing to look expectantly at me. It
got to the point where I refused to make eye contact with
her.

I'd been there ten minutes, nursing what was in my cup,
when somebody slid onto the stool beside me.

"Roxie said you were looking for me."

I swiveled on my seat and found a balding man wearing
a shirt with metal collar tips, a bolo tie and the gaudiest
cowboy boots I'd ever seen in my life. "Mr. Graybill?"

"You can call me Marty; everybody does," he said as he
stuck out his hand.

I took it, then said, "Nice place you've got here."

"Thank you kindly, sir. Now what can I do for you?"

I took a sip of coffee, then said, "I'm here to talk to you
about Gretel Barnett."

Marty stiffened slightly beside me, then said, "Don't
know much about her. She was new in town. It's a shame
what happened to her."

"That's a pretty charitable attitude, considering that you must have been pretty upset with her."

His "boy howdy" attitude was slipping quickly. "Why do you say that?"

"I've talked to Runion, I know all about the deal she blew for all of you."

Marty suddenly didn't seem all that friendly anymore. "We're doing fine here. I'm not even sure I was going to sell myself. I'm happy running this restaurant."

"That's not what I heard. So where were you last Saturday?"

He looked at me like he'd just bitten into a lemon. "You're asking me for an alibi? The way I hear it, you're the one who shot her."

I felt an icy chill. "So you know who I am."

"Son, everybody in the county knows your mug after that spread they did on you in the newspaper."

"The police know that I didn't kill her," I said, a statement that was more optimistic than I felt. "They're looking for alternate suspects now."

Marty said, "I'll answer to them, but I won't answer to you."

It was time to nudge him a little. "So you do have something to hide."

He got up, leaned over me and said, "Not that it's any of your business, but I was right here, just like every other Saturday since I've owned this place. It's our busiest day, and no one gets off; not even me. I've got to go."

After he'd disappeared, I waved the waitress over. She said, "Are you ready now, Sugar?"

"Just the check," I said.

She scribbled out something on a pad, then slipped it to me. I left her a tip, a lot bigger than she merited, then took my bill to the register. The redhead was ringing someone up ahead of me, and when she got to me, I said, "Thanks for pointing Marty my way."

"You're welcome," she said as she took my money.

"I heard you'all were selling the place," I said as casually as I could manage it.

"He was going to, but the deal fell through. Marty hasn't been the same since." She lowered her voice and added, "I shouldn't say anything, but we're just squeaking by here. Marty always wanted to move out West, and he was afraid this was his last chance."

I was about to ask something else when Marty suddenly reappeared. "Roxie, I need you in the office."

"But Thelma's on break. Somebody's got to run the register."

"Let Shelly do it. Now, Roxie."

She handed me my change, then walked back to Marty. He didn't say another word to me, but his glare was smoking as I left.

As I walked outside, I thought about how casual Marty had tried to play me, and how earnest he'd really been about selling out, according to Roxie. I hoped she didn't get in trouble for leveling with me, but I was glad she'd been forthright. Marty Graybill could stand a little more scrutiny. Even though he claimed he'd been working all Saturday, it shouldn't be all that hard to check. I'd have to leave that to Morton, though. He had the resources to follow up on alibis. All I could do was point the sheriff in the right direction. Morton and I were going to have to have a long talk soon. I had to come up with some way to share what I'd learned without stepping on his toes. It was going to have to be a delicate dance, but I'd done it before.

I had some time on my hands before I had to get to the candleshop for my shift, so I walked down the block toward Flickering Lights. I wanted to see if Jubal had been able to track down Gretel's brother. As I walked down the street, I saw FOR RENT signs in three of the buildings along the way. These were most likely Mrs. Jorgenson's properties and the Minnesota investor. At least Marty Graybill was generating income from his restaurant. The two of them were losing money every day their buildings stood empty. I still couldn't see Mrs. Jorgenson as a killer, and I promised myself I'd make another stab at patching things up with her. Maybe after I spoke with Jubal, I'd drive back out to her place and try to get an audience.

Jubal was alone in his shop, a sign I hoped meant that my customers were starting to come back to me. "Harrison, good of you to come by. Is your candleshop closed this morning?"

"No, I've got an assistant running it when I'm not there."

He sighed. "It's an incredible amount of work, operating a shop by yourself, isn't it? It's no wonder Gretel invited me down here to work with her. Frankly, I'm not sure how much longer I can keep the place open."

"What about Hans? Has anyone heard from him?"

"The attorney tells me he's doing everything in his power to locate him, but to be honest with you, I don't know how much luck he's going to have. Hans never was my favorite. I'd walk through fire for Gretel, but her brother is a different story entirely. Greed ruled him."

"Do me a favor, Jubal. If you do hear from him, would you let me know?"

"More idle speculation, Harrison? I was under the impression that things were quieting down."

"What makes you say that?" I asked.

He picked up a copy of *The Gunpowder Gazette*. "It's more what they're not saying than what they're printing. You haven't been mentioned in days."

"I suppose that's something to be thankful for, anyway." I glanced at my watch and realized that if I was going to have time to drive out to Mrs. Jorgenson's before my shift started, I'd have to get going.

As I headed for the door, I said, "Remember, call me if you hear from him."

Jubal nodded and I left him to his candleshop.

Mrs. Jorgenson's car was nowhere in sight when I pulled up in front of her house, though she had a huge garage that was a completely separate building. I walked over and tried to peek inside, but the tinting was so dark I couldn't see a thing. Her butler must have noticed my arrival, because he opened the door before I'd even had the chance to knock.

"I'm afraid Mrs. Jorgenson is still unavailable."

"Come on, I just want a few words with her."

"So sorry," he said, then closed the door on me.

So much for the direct approach. I had no doubt she was in there somewhere, but if I was going to make amends, I was going to have to find another way to do it than face to face.

I drove back to At Wick's End wondering how I was going to manage that. By the time I got back, I was no closer to an answer than I'd been before. I went upstairs to my apartment and made a quick sandwich, then headed down to the candleshop for my shift.

Eve met me at the door, breathless. "Harrison Black, where have you been?"

"I'm not due to come in until noon. Didn't you look at the schedule?"

She said, "I know that, but it was an awful time to be away from the shop."

"Oh no. What did I miss?" It seemed like the few times I left the shop to Eve, something happened that needed my attention. I wasn't about to stay there around the clock, though. Soon after I'd taken over all of River's Edge, I'd learned my time away from the place was important for me to maintain my sanity. I could well sympathize with Jubal's fatigue at working every hour his shop was open.

Eve said, "Mrs. Jorgenson came by an hour ago. She was quite upset that she'd missed you."

"I was at her place trying to get past her butler. Did she say what she wanted?"

Eve shook her head. "No, all she would say was that she'd talk to you some other time."

"How did she act?" I asked.

"Harrison, you know it's impossible to tell that woman's mood from her expression or behavior. She's always so stone-faced it's a wonder she doesn't freeze like that."

I'd seen a few cracks in that façade since I'd started teaching her candlemaking, but even I had to admit they were rare in their appearances.

She studied me a moment, then asked, "So what are you going to do?"

"Eve, there's nothing I can do. I've tried to get past her butler, but he won't budge. She knows where I am. I apologized, I even gave her that basket you made up, though she tried to get the butler to give it back to me. I don't know what else I can do."

"Harrison Black, you're as stubborn as she is."

I grinned, "Yeah, but I'm not as stubborn as Belle was. Give me time, though. I'm working on it."

Eve snorted loudly, then said, "I'm going to lunch."

While she was gone, the foot traffic in the candleshop picked up considerably. By the time she got back, I was in a deep discussion with a woman about incising candles with dimensional designs and overdipping. The woman purchased a set of carving knives and some different wax tints, and after she was gone, Eve said, "My, you've come a long way, Harrison. I didn't know you'd learned to incise candles."

I showed her a round white candle I'd overdipped in red wax, then scribed feathery crystals into the surface. "I made this last week." It had actually been much easier to create the effect than it appeared. I had always enjoyed drawing, and etching the surface of the red wax to expose the white beneath it was the same technique as drawing, just in a different medium.

Eve took the sample from me, studied it in the light, then said, "You may have gone a little deep here." She pointed to a slight gouge. "And you should have brushed this wax away after you scribed it," she added as she pointed out an errant hint of white.

Before I could reply, she said, "Otherwise, it's a perfect job."

"Thanks," I said, happy to get any compliment on my candlemaking from her, even if it was a backhanded one. We worked together until five, then Eve prepared to go home. I was staying open until seven that evening, and while I didn't particularly care to work the shop alone, getting a morning off now and then more than made up for the inconvenience.

Ten minutes after she was gone, Sheriff Morton walked in, and from the sour expression on his face, I knew he wasn't there to make a social call.

"Where's Pearly?" he said without salutation.

"Still in the mountains," I said. "And how are you today, Sheriff?"

"Save it, Harrison, I'm not in the mood for your glib comments. I need to find your handyman."

"Like I told you before, he's away on vacation. What's the sense of urgency?"

Morton frowned. "The headline from *The Gunpowder Gazette* tomorrow is going to name Pearly as my chief suspect. It's going to be kind of embarrassing if I don't know where he is, now isn't it?"

"Is the *Gazette* running the sheriff's office now?"

Morton got up in my face and said hotly, "You might want to watch yourself."

I took a step back. "Sorry, that was out of line. Who told them Pearly was even on your list?"

"You're not the only one digging into this besides me. Don't even try to look shocked or outraged; I've heard what you've been doing around town."

"Sheriff, can you really blame me? I've been trying to clear my name."

"I never named you a suspect," Morton said.

"You didn't have to. The newspaper did that without your help. What did they find out?"

"Somebody leaked Gretel's bequest to Pearly. That, added to the fact that they'd just broken up and Pearly was spotted at the fair, makes for a pretty solid case."

"Surely you don't believe it," I said.

"Love and greed can be a pretty powerful combination," Morton said. "I need to talk to him, Harrison."

"Sorry, but I don't know where he is. Believe me or don't, but it's the truth."

Morton frowned at me again, then slammed the door to the candleshop on his way out. There hadn't been anything I could do to protect Pearly. Even if I'd known where he was, I wouldn't have told the sheriff, though. I would have warned my handyman to stay out of town as long as he could. I knew firsthand what the scrutiny of an article in the *Gazette* could bring, and I didn't envy him the experience.

Millie walked in and said, "Thank goodness, you're still here."

"Why would you think otherwise?"

She said, "I saw the sheriff drive up, but I was with a customer when he left. I just thought . . . you know, that something might have happened."

"No, he didn't arrest me, but he probably wanted to. He's after Pearly, though. There's going to be an article in tomorrow's paper about him, and the sheriff wants to find him first."

"Poor Pearly," she said.

"I made the mistake of saying the newspaper was running the sheriff's department. I thought he was going to arrest me on the spot."

Millie said, "You probably shouldn't have done that."

"I know, but who knew he'd be so touchy?"

"During the last election, there were complaints that Morton received too much press, and that Coburn was barely mentioned at all, even though he was the incumbent. The sheriff's been kind of touchy since then."

"Wonderful. I seem to always manage to say exactly the wrong thing."

"You couldn't know, Harrison. So what are we going to do about Pearly?" She picked up the candle I'd shown Eve and spun it in her hands.

"We can hope he stays away until this blows over," I said.

"We've got to do more than that. Harrison, you need to get to the bottom of this. You're good at puzzles. You should look into this."

"I've been so busy trying to clear my own name, I haven't had time to think about Pearly."

Millie said, "Well, you'd better start. We can't lose him, Harrison; he's the glue that holds this place together."

"I'll do what I can," I said.

She studied the candle a moment more, then put it back on the display table. "That's a lovely candle. Was it one of Belle's?"

"I made it myself," I admitted.

"My, you're getting quite good at it."

I picked the candle up and handed it to her.

She said, "What's this?"

"Accept it as a token of my friendship and appreciation," I said.

"Oh, Harrison, I can't do that. You sell these."

"And you sell your muffins, Pan Dowdies and everything else you let me sample. Come on, Millie, it would mean a lot to me."

She nodded. "Thank you, Harrison. I'll display it on my counter, and tell everyone where I got it."

I laughed. "Hey, I wasn't looking for free advertising."

"Just consider it a bonus, then."

After she was gone, I worked until closing selling a few supplies but barely making enough to pay the electric bill. At least there was enough to deposit, something I wouldn't have bet on a few days earlier. I made out the slip, locked the candleshop and drove into town to get the money into the bank's night deposit. While I was in town, I decided to swing by Erin's on the off chance she was in. Unfortunately, the lights were off at her rental place, and though we'd been building something, a friendship or a budding relationship or what I wasn't sure, I wasn't ready to just show up on her doorstep.

There was someone I could visit unannounced, though.

When I pulled into Wayne's driveway, I was happy to see his car parked there. With his new girlfriend, he hadn't had much time for me, but it looked like I was in luck.

I had to ring the doorbell twice before he answered.

"Hey, what's up? Did we have something planned tonight?" he asked.

"No, I just thought I'd drop in and grace you with my presence. Come on, there's got to be some kind of game somewhere on television. Let's watch it."

In the background, I heard a woman's voice calling out, "Wayne? Who is it?"

I started to back away. "Sorry, I should have called first."

"No, it's all right," he said. "Come on in. You really should meet Nichole."

"Another time," I said as I headed back to my truck.

"Sorry," he called out.

"Not a problem."

Of course I should have realized he'd be with his new girlfriend. I drove back to River's Edge and decided to find that game on television myself. That all changed suddenly, though. As I drove up to the complex, I saw a light burning in one of the windows that had no business being on.

Twelve

"I didn't realize you were still around," I said to Heather after she let me into her shop.

"I had some cleaning to do," she said, looking toward the back of her store, The New Age. At that moment, we both heard something fall.

"Is there somebody back there?" I asked. "Or is it just Esmeralda?"

"It must be," she said. "Wait right here and I'll go get her. I know she'll be thrilled to see you."

"How would we be able to tell?" I asked. "She's never shown the slightest interest in whether I'm around or not, unless it's mealtime and I'm the one feeding her."

"Come on, Harrison, admit it. You and my cat have a special bond."

"Heather, if it helps you sleep better at night believing it, good for you." I started toward the back of the store when Esme herself trotted out. Proving my point, she ignored me completely and leapt into Heather's arms.

I added, "Oh, she's absolutely devoted to me. You were right all along." I reached out slowly, then scratched Esmeralda under her chin. She purred softly, moving her neck until I had the precise spot she wanted. She would have probably stayed like that for the rest of the night, but I wasn't going to spend it catering to her whims.

Heather said, "Honestly, I don't know why you're afraid to express any affection for my cat."

I looked directly at Esmeralda and said to her, "You're not the worst roommate I've ever had in my life."

Heather laughed, then said, "See, Esme? He does care."

Esmeralda seemed singularly unimpressed by it all.

It was time to change this particular subject. "Are you finished up here, or do you have much more to do? I could help, if you need a hand."

"You spend too much time around the complex as it is. You deserve a life of your own, Harrison."

"Yeah, well, that's open for debate. So what do you say? If we both dig in, we can have your cleaning done in half the time."

She frowned, then said, "You know what? There's nothing that needs to be done here that can't wait until tomorrow. Why don't you buy me a drink?"

"I guess I could."

"Gee, your enthusiasm is underwhelming."

"I was just thinking we could go upstairs instead. I've got some wine chilling in the fridge, and there's beer if you prefer that."

She said, "Harrison Black, are you trying to take advantage of me, say, by plying me with alcohol?"

"No, Ma'am, I'm a Southern Gentleman. If you're not in the mood to be plied, I won't try. I promise."

She laughed, then said, "Just in case, I think I'll bring Esmeralda along as our chaperone."

"That's a dandy idea. You can never be too careful these days."

After locking up her store, we headed upstairs and I opened my apartment door. Esme squirmed out of Heather's arms and ran inside. I called out, "Don't get too comfortable, you're not staying over this time."

What a surprise; Esme ignored me completely.

Heather looked around and said, "I just love what you've done with the place. Honestly, Harrison, don't you ever get tired of candles? They're everywhere."

I looked around at the candles scattered through the apartment. There were botched and more successful attempts of mine on display from more experiments than I could name. I'd managed to butcher techniques in pouring, rolling, gelling, dripping, molding, flaring, twisting, marbling and incising candles in my attempts to perfect my newfound trade. I was in the process of burning my failures; it gave me real satisfaction that even if some of my efforts weren't the most beautiful candles ever made, they still gave off light, and in many cases, aromas that brought back memories I'd thought I'd lost long ago. "I don't know, I think it looks just about right."

She laughed and asked as she picked up one of my latest efforts, "What happened here? Did you run out of wax?"

I plucked the candle out of her hands. "Hey, that's one of my better ice candles."

"Candles and ice? You're kidding, right?"

"Trust me, this is really a cool process. You take a dipped taper and put it in the center of a cylindrical mold. Then you arrange the ice chips in the mold around it and pour the hot wax in. It's not nearly as tough as it looks."

"So you say," Heather said.

"It's the truth," I said. "Take it, burn it, enjoy it." After all, I'd given Millie a candle earlier. One of the best things about making candles was sharing them with the people around me. Heather didn't even put up token resistance. "I love it, but it's too pretty to burn."

"Candles are meant to be enjoyed. Tell you what. You burn this one, and next time I'll teach you how to make one of your own."

"It's a deal," she said.

"How about that drink now?" I asked her.

"To be honest with you, what I'd really like is a cup of tea."

I raised an eyebrow. "Now how am I supposed to get you liquored up if you won't drink?"

"You'll just have to rely on your charm," she said with a laugh.

"Then I'm in trouble. I'll put the kettle on to boil; tea sounds good to me, too." As I did, I asked Heather, "Where's that delinquent cat of yours? I've learned from experience that she causes the most trouble whenever she's quiet."

Heather pointed to one of the bookcases and said, "She's watching you."

I nodded. "I've been told I bear watching."

We were just settling down to our cups of tea when there was a knock on my door. I half-expected Markum to pop his head inside.

Instead, Becka was in the hallway. "Hi, Harrison. Do you have a second?" She looked past me and saw Heather inside. "Sorry to bother you. I didn't realize you had company."

"Nonsense, come on in."

"Heather said, "I was just leaving, anyway."

"You don't have to go on my account."

I looked at Heather and said, "You're more than welcome to stay."

She shook her head. "I'd really better be going, Harrison. Let me collect Esme and I'll be on my way."

"Are you sure you have to go?"

She looked at Becka, who was intently studying her hands, then said, "I'd better. We'll talk again tomorrow."

She scooped Esme off the shelf, then said, "Thanks again for the tea."

She was nearly to the door when I said, "Hey, don't forget your candle."

Heather took it from me, then kissed me lightly on the cheek. "That was so thoughtful of you."

"I was happy to do it."

Heather nodded toward Becka, then she and Esme left. She'd been gone two minutes when Becka said, "I'm sorry about just barging in like that. I didn't realize you were dating anyone, Harrison."

"Heather has the shop downstairs beside mine. We're just friends."

Becka perked up at the news, so I added quickly, "Just like the two of us are."

"But we used to be so much more," she said.

"The key part of that sentence is 'used to.'"

Becka stared at me a few seconds, then said, "Are you trying to be mean, or does it just come naturally?"

Before I could say another word, she stormed off into my bathroom and slammed the door.

Now what had I said to bring that on? If she was laboring under the misimpression that we were ever going to date again, the sooner I dispelled that notion the better. I'd had more than enough of her prima donna behavior in the past to ever put up with it again.

After a few minutes, Becka came back out, acting as if nothing had happened.

I stretched and stifled a yawn. "I hate to be rude, but I'm really worn out."

"I can take a hint as well as the next gal," Becka said. She started to kiss my cheek, just as Heather had, then changed her mind at the last second and offered me her hand. I took it lightly, then held the door open for her.

"Good night," I said.

"Bye," she called out and headed down the steps to the exit.

After Becka was gone, I decided I'd had enough excitement for one night. I grabbed a quick bite, then headed off to bed to read. I worried about Pearly, with a likely arrest looming the second he got back to Micah's Ridge. But there was nothing I could do to help him, no matter how much he needed it.

And it killed me to admit it.

EVE AND I were working the morning shift together the next day when I heard the chime go off over the front door. To my surprise, it was Mrs. Jorgenson. Eve was right. I couldn't tell from the expression on her face whether she was there to hug me or slap me with a lawsuit.

"Harrison, I'd like to speak with you."

"Absolutely. What's on your mind?"

She looked around the candleshop, and though we were alone except for Eve, Mrs. Jorgenson said, "I'd rather have this conversation away from the shop."

I had no idea what that meant. "Fine. We can go to The Crocked Pot for a cup of coffee." I started to tell Eve, but she just nodded her approval.

Mrs. Jorgenson said, "I'm sure it will be acceptable."

We walked outside and down the front promenade toward Millie's place. The wind was gusting slightly, just enough to raise some of the flags displayed in front of the shops. I'd found a flag place going out of business and had bought several themed flags for my tenants. There was a single white candle on a field of red in front of my shop, while Millie's had a coffee cup, Sanora's pottery sported a vase and Suzanne Gladstone's antique shop had a rocking chair on it. Heather's had been a problem, but I'd finally settled on a brightly colored rainbow for her. She'd been delighted with the choice, and I had to admit, the banners waving in the wind did give all of River's Edge more of a whimsical look. I'd thought about it for some time before making any changes to my late great-aunt Belle's place, but in the end I was the one responsible for how the complex looked, and if something would help in any way, I was all for it as long as I could afford it.

If Mrs. Jorgenson noticed the banners, or anything else that morning, she didn't say.

"What would you like?" Millie asked Mrs. Jorgenson when we walked into the café.

"Something more mundane than your exotic choices," she said, studying the menu.

"I'll take care of this," I said. "Why don't you find us a table and I'll be right with you."

Mrs. Jorgenson found a spot away from the few customers already there. She was serious about keeping our conversation private.

Millie looked expectantly at me, so I ordered two plain coffees. As she filled the order, she said, "She's lovely, Harrison, honestly she is, but I think you can do better. She's awfully old for you, isn't she?"

I whispered, "This isn't a date, you nit. That's Mrs. Jorgenson."

Millie had heard all about the craft queen benefactress. "So that's Mrs. J in the flesh. I take it you've managed to bring her back into your fold?"

"I have no idea. That's why we're here."

Millie added a small plate and put two biscotti on it.

"Hey, I didn't order these."

"They're on the house. Maybe they'll loosen her up."

"It's going to take a lot more than that," I whispered.

I carried the coffees and cookies to the table and slid one mug in front of Mrs. Jorgenson. She looked at the plate for a moment, then said, "I didn't ask for this."

"It's on the house," I said.

Still staring at the plate, she said, "I don't approve of dessert."

"I do," I said. "So it's no problem. I'll eat them both. Now what is it that you wanted to talk to me about?"

"Blunt, direct and to the point. I see this ordeal hasn't changed your basic personality traits."

"Mrs. Jorgenson, I've tried to be charming with you. It didn't work, remember? Seriously, though, I would like to know why you're here, especially after your man Jeeves slammed the door in my face."

Was that the crack of a smile I saw? I couldn't be certain; it had vanished too quickly. She said, "His name's Henderson, actually, and he's quite important to me."

"I'm happy for you both. I know one thing: he certainly keeps the riffraff away. I just didn't realize that included me."

Mrs. Jorgenson frowned at me, then at her coffee, then back at me. "I knew this was going to be difficult. However, I didn't realize you'd be exacerbating the situation."

She was right. "Okay, I'm sorry. I'll try to be good. I promise."

She took a sip of her coffee, smiled in a surprised way, then said, "First of all, I believe I owe you an apology."

"I owe you one too, so I guess that makes us even."

She raised an eyebrow pointedly, then said, "Would you please let me finish?"

I nodded, and somehow managed to keep my mouth shut.

She continued, "I never should have reacted the way I did with you. Was I frustrated that the sale of those buildings was scuttled because of that woman's stubbornness? Absolutely. She was never supposed to have a chance to purchase that property in the first place. I'd put a preemptive bid with the previous owner, but it appeared that Mrs. Barnett was more persuasive than I was with him. But in all honesty, I wasn't even inconvenienced by her balking on the deal. That property's in a prime location. By waiting, it might actually result in a higher profit for me and the other owners. I certainly didn't shoot anyone, particularly at something called a Founder's Day Fair."

"It was called a Founder's Day Celebration," I said, correcting her.

"Harrison, I wouldn't have cared if it had been dubbed the Winter Cotillion, I still wouldn't have attended. Street fairs are not events I regularly choose as entertainment." She took another sip of coffee, then added, "I overreacted, I admit it. You were looking for information, not slinging accusations. I'm afraid I was a bit hasty lashing out at you like that. I apologize."

I doubted she had apologized to more than four people in the last twenty years. "We're even, then. I shouldn't have been so persistent questioning you. It's a character flaw of mine."

"There's nothing flawed about going after what you

want. I just wasn't used to being a murder suspect in anybody's mind."

I finished my coffee, then said, "So we're both sorry for the way we've acted lately. Where does that leave us? Do you have any interest in pursuing your candlemaking lessons with me?"

She looked startled by the question. "Yes, of course I do. That's why I'm here."

Finally, some good news. "That's great. I've been working on some new techniques for overdipping and incising that I think you're going to love." I glanced at my watch. "I don't have anything ready now, but give me an hour and I can set some things up."

"I'm afraid I'll have to say no," she said.

"Was there something else you wanted to study first?"

She said, "It's not that. I just don't have the time for anything so lengthy." She saw my disappointment, though to be fair I hadn't tried that hard to hide it. I not only liked the cash infusion from Mrs. Jorgenson's lessons—they made me feel like a real candlemaker—but passing on my knowledge almost as fast as I gained it was extremely rewarding.

She looked at her watch, paused a moment, then said, "Do you have anything quick we can do? Something that won't take long but that is still a legitimate type of candlemaking?"

"I've got just the thing. We can make gel candles. They aren't hard at all, especially after what you've tackled so far. I'm afraid you'd be bored doing them."

"Let me be the judge of that, young man. Lead the way."

Thirteen

WHEN Mrs. Jorgenson and I walked through the door of At Wick's End together, Eve looked as though she hadn't expected either of us back anytime soon.

I told my student, "If you'll go back to the classroom, I'll be right with you."

Mrs. Jorgenson nodded, then said, "Don't be long. I've barely got time for a lesson as it is."

"I'll grab a kit and we'll get started."

She said, "No more kits, Harrison. Let's do this one on our own, shall we?"

I nodded. "Good enough. Give me two minutes and I'll be ready."

After she walked back to the small classroom, I grabbed a round tub of gel wax, a handful of prewaxed wicks two inches long and half a dozen small glass containers. Eve abandoned her customer and came over to me. "What are you doing?"

"Mrs. J wants a lesson, so I thought I'd oblige her."

"Gel candles, Harrison? Don't you think they might be a little too easy for your expert student?"

"Hey, don't blame me, it was her idea. Do you want to tell her she's advanced too far to make these? Eve, they're fun to do, and they are a legitimate way to make candles. She doesn't have much time, so I'd better get going."

Eve said, "Make it good, Harrison."

I smiled. "Don't I always? You worry too much."

I found Mrs. Jorgenson looking through some of our bins that housed candlemaking extras. She was looking at a tray of semiprecious stones I'd bought in Hiddenite after accompanying Heather on her last crystal-buying trip there. While the rocks weren't worth much, they made dandy candle additions, and I'd even made a few for sale with rewarding results. I said, "Grab what you like and we can use them in your candles."

She started to choose a few stones, particularly a flawed amethyst that I liked, then put them back. "You know I don't like to add things to my candles until I've learned the basic techniques."

"Well, this is pretty straightforward. We melt the gel we need, then arrange our accessories and pour in the wax."

"That's all?" she asked.

"You can make it much more complicated. I've made some sea floor scenes with sand and shells, and I made one with a light blue tint and added tiny airplanes for a birthday party. It's fun, you'll like it." I added, "Hang on a second, let me get you a few of my examples."

I dashed out front, grabbed some of the gel candles I'd made recently and brought them back in. As I walked back to the classroom, I saw Eve waiting on the woman with the frosted beehive hairdo again and found myself wondering where I'd seen her besides the candleshop. There was no time to pursue it at the moment, but it was still driving me crazy.

I showed Mrs. J the samples. She studied them for a minute, then said, "Why are there varying amounts of bubbles?"

"That's one of the neat things about this technique. It's all based on the temperature of the gel when you pour it. You get a lot more bubbles at a hundred and eighty degrees than you do at two-ten. The bubbles are almost entirely eliminated then."

"So why don't you heat the wax to two hundred and fifty degrees and make it clear?"

I shrugged and said, "I've heard that you can preheat the container in an oven, but I haven't tried it myself. I do know that if you get the wax too hot, you'll scorch it." I knew from experience how closely you had to watch the temperature on the thermometer to be sure you didn't overheat it.

Mrs. Jorgenson didn't say anything, but she began collecting a handful of smaller stones, and on a whim she added a small piece of birch bark.

"Okay, now let's heat the wax, and you can make your layout plan while it's melting," I told her.

I opened the tub and showed her what the gel wax looked like in its container. She touched it tentatively, then pulled back her finger. "It's not at all what I expected. It's so rubbery."

"When it's heated, it will be totally liquid," I said. The first time I'd made gel candles, I'd heated the wax in a double boiler, but that took forever. I learned it worked fine in a regular pan, and had the advantage of being a lot quicker.

"Now, while that's melting," I said, "let's pick out a few containers for you. Would you like to add a color?" I asked, knowing that Mrs. Jorgenson would never go for it. She believed the basics had to be mastered before anything extra could be added.

She shocked me by saying, "Why not? How about some red?"

"That's the spirit," I said, grabbing a small chunk of the red dye.

Mrs. Jorgenson said, "Can we add it after we've poured the first one? I'd like to have one of each."

"Mrs. Jorgenson, we can do whatever you'd like." As the wax started to melt, I stirred it a little, then checked the temperature with one of our thermometers.

"We're at a hundred and eighty-five," I said.

She looked at her watch, then said, "Oh, dear, I can't wait much longer. Can we pour now?"

"If you don't mind the bubbles, we're ready," I said.

"Bubbles are fine. Let's pour."

I transferred the gel wax into a container with a spout, then handed it to her. "Now just pour the wax around the wick. It's okay if you get some wax on it, it will peel right off. That's good," I said as she made her pour.

Mrs. Jorgenson handed the pot back to me, and I poured it back into the pan. The gel wax quickly liquefied again, and I handed the dye to my pupil. "Go ahead and put it in."

"There's not much here," she said.

"Remember, a little goes a long way."

Once it was ready, I transferred it yet again into the pouring container and she quickly had a second candle.

"What do we do now?" she asked.

"Give it a little time to set up, then you're ready to burn it."

She studied the top of the second candle and said, "It's rather bumpy, isn't it?"

I pulled out a hair dryer and said, "Just give it a quick shot from this and it will be fine."

She did as I suggested, and the candle's top evened out. "That's amazing."

"Just a trick of the trade," I said. "It's a shame you don't have time to do any more."

"I agree. Do you have any kits I can take with me?" she said, her earlier complaint about kits quickly forgotten. "You've shown me the technique, so I can practice at home on my own." I set her up with two of our deluxe gel kits while she collected several bags of items to include in her candles. Eve rang the sale up gratefully, but she didn't let her breath out until Mrs. Jorgenson was gone.

"Man, oh man, that was too close," I said. "For a minute there at the start, I thought I was going to lose her."

"Harrison, I can't believe she came back. What did you say to her?"

"We both apologized, and after that, she was raring to go again. I noticed you had a few customers while I was teaching."

Eve said, "I made a few little sales, but nothing big. Jubal Grant came by."

"What did he want?"

"I'm not quite sure. He said it wasn't important. If you want to know the truth, I think the poor man's lonely. You appear to be the only soul he knows in Micah's Ridge."

"That very well could be. I'll try to stop by and see him sometime in the next few days. Hey, I noticed that our frosted beehive lady was back," I said. "I know her from somewhere, but I can't put my finger on it for the life of me." I stared off into space for a few minutes, then suddenly it hit me. "I've got it," I said a little too loudly. "She was at the Founder's Day celebration. In fact, I spotted her talking to Gretel just before she was shot."

"So she likes candles. It makes sense that she'd talk to two chandlers, wouldn't it? Harrison, you're getting paranoid again."

"No, I'm saying she was right there when Gretel went down. She might have seen something. I need to talk to her."

I ran out the door and scanned the other shops when I saw she wasn't in the parking lot, but it was too late; she was already gone.

I told Eve she had vanished, then headed over to Millie's for lunch. Normally I ducked upstairs to grab a quick sandwich, but I wasn't in the mood to be alone. Millie's place was crowded, but I found a spot by the front window after I ordered my meal. I was sipping a Coke when I nearly choked on the drink. The woman with the frosted beehive hairdo I was looking for came out of Millie's bathroom and headed toward the counter.

I approached her and asked, "Excuse me, but do you have a minute? I'd really like to talk to you. I'd be happy to buy you a cup of coffee, or even lunch."

"You're from the candleshop, right," she said, studying me curiously.

"At Wick's End, that's right. My name's Harrison Black."

"Mr. Black, I'm flattered, I really am, but I'm afraid I'm not interested. It isn't you. You're just not my type."

"Ma'am, I promise you I'm not trying to pick you up. I just want to ask you a few questions."

She said, "Surely it's not about candlemaking."

"Please? If you don't want to eat with me, give me two minutes of your time and I'll leave you alone."

She thought another moment, then turned to Millie and

ordered the most expensive combo on the menu. "Put it on his bill," she said.

With what her lobster salad sandwich was costing me, I hoped the woman had some answers for me. Millie raised one eyebrow, but I nodded my agreement to the deal.

"First off," I said as soon as we were at my table, "I don't know your name."

"I'm Evelyn," she said. "No last names. You can't be too careful these days."

"Evelyn's fine." I took a sip of Coke, then said, "I saw you at the Founder's Day Celebration the day Gretel died. In fact, you were standing right beside her."

"Are you accusing me of something, Mr. Black?"

"No, of course not," I said, though if the sheriff's forensic team had found powder burns on Gretel's back, I would have. "I was just wondering if you saw anything."

"I saw a great many things that day, and heard even more," she said. "Of course you mean when that poor woman was shot. I was quite shaken when I saw her collapse. You were nearby yourself, weren't you? Did you hear the shot? I didn't, but there were so many dreadful fireworks going on that day it's a wonder we're not all deaf."

"So you didn't see anything?"

She said, "I wouldn't go that far. You saw the clown too, didn't you?"

"Clown? What are you talking about?"

"Standing just to the side of you was a man in clown makeup. He had on a red and blue suit and wore those ridiculous floppy shoes, too. I thought it odd that he had one of those toy guns that said BANG on a piece of cloth unfurled from the barrel just after that poor woman was shot. Quite inappropriate, if you ask me."

"I missed him," I admitted. "I was more focused on Gretel falling."

"He was standing right beside the cannon, I don't know how you could have missed him."

"Did you tell the police what you saw?"

She said, "I tried, but the moment I mentioned the clown, the deputy I was speaking with got an odd look on his face, as if he were trying not to laugh. Well, sir, I know when I'm being mocked. I wasn't about to just stand there and take it."

"I don't suppose you could identify this clown if you saw him again, could you?"

"Mr. Black, are you making fun of me as well?" she asked as she started to rise out of her chair.

"No, Ma'am, I just remember reading that most clowns like to stick to a particular design in their makeup. I was just wondering what this clown's face looked like."

"They really are evil, aren't they, always mocking us," she said. "This one had teardrops running down each cheek, and a huge frown painted across his mouth. That's all I remember. Honestly, I shouldn't even have been there in the first place, but I went by Flickering Lights and they were closed."

"Are you sure about that?" I asked.

"Now Mr. Black, to be fair, I didn't even know about At Wick's End. I just moved to Micah's Ridge."

I waved a hand in the air. "I'm not worried about where you were shopping. I thought Flickering Lights was open all day Saturday."

"I'm sure the store was open at some point, but I must have caught Mr. Grant on his lunch hour. I knew Gretel was operating a booth, so I decided to drive over to New Conover on the spur of the moment."

I fully realized that there were businesses that closed

during lunch, especially on Saturdays, but Jubal had claimed to have worked through his lunch hour that day. Had he lied to me, or had he stepped into the restroom for a discreet break, unwilling to leave the candleshop unattended for even a few moments? Or perhaps he'd stepped out for a bite and didn't want to admit that he'd closed the shop. I envied him the ability to do it if that was the case, but it just highlighted the differences between working at a store and owning it. When I'd first taken over At Wick's End, I was reticent to even close the place down at night, and it was obvious from my conversations with Jubal that candlemaking wasn't a passion for him.

Our food came before I had the chance to ask any more questions, and once that sandwich was in front of Evelyn, she lost all interest in talking to me. It was amazing watching her devour her order. It took me a few minutes to remember my own sandwich, lying half-forgotten on my plate.

When she'd finished, Evelyn said, "That was wonderful. I've been dying to try it since I first came here. Thank you, Mr. Black."

I couldn't believe she'd taken advantage of me like that, but there was nothing left to do but be gracious about the whole thing. "You're most welcome. I have another question. Would you be willing to talk to the police again about this clown you saw?"

She stood and said, "I doubt it. What do you expect me to do, pick him out of a lineup? Come now, he was in full makeup. I wouldn't know the man if he walked up to me on the street and slapped me in the face with a dead fish."

"What makes you think it was a man?" I asked.

"Come now, it was a general expression." She started

for the door, then paused and looked back at me. "Actually, I'm fairly certain it was a man. He had an average build, but there was something about the way he carried himself that made me assume his gender. I'm truly sorry I couldn't be more help to you."

She bolted out the door before I had the chance to ask her anything else. Millie came over to bus our table, and as she stacked the plastic baskets on top of one another, she said, "I don't even want to know what that was about."

I shook my head and said, "Good, because I wouldn't know where to begin to tell you."

Millie said, "Wrong answer, my friend. How am I supposed to live with not knowing why you bought that dreadful woman lunch?"

"Do you know her?" I asked.

"She comes around for the soup of the day, my dollar ninety-nine special, then cleans out my cracker supply. Whooee, she saw you coming, didn't she?" Millie cleaned off the tabletop with a damp rag, then said, "You're not dating her too, are you?"

"Come on, give me more credit than that."

"So why the free lunch?" she asked.

"She was at the fair when Gretel died," I said as Heather walked in.

"Who was?" she asked as she joined us.

"Nobody," I said. "It's not important."

Millie said, "Heather, I've got your sandwiches ready."

As she went to get them, I said, "Did she say plural? Don't tell me you're taking somebody else out to lunch yourself." Heather and I shared a picnic lunch occasionally on the concrete steps that led from the River's Edge complex down to the water of the Gunpowder River. Since the weather had turned cold, we hadn't had any outdoor feasts, but there was no doubt we'd renew the habit once things warmed up.

"I can't wait around forever for an invitation from you," she said with a smile.

"So who's the lucky lunch mate?"

She said, "Sorry, it's not all that exciting. I may be working late tonight, so I thought I'd get something for the fridge. I keep plenty of Esme's food on hand; I don't know why I can't keep things around for myself."

"Bon appétit," Millie said. "I hope you enjoy both meals."

"Thanks," she said distractedly as she took the bags from her. The residents of River's Edge all kept a tab with Millie and settled up at the end of the month. It was handy for us that way and easier for her to collect it all at once. After she was gone, Millie said, "That was odd."

"I know, I thought she was buying lunch for somebody else, but she explained that one sandwich was for now and the other was for later."

Millie nodded, "I guess that explains it. But who in their right mind would want to eat the same meal twice in a row?"

"You're kidding, right? If they were your sandwiches, I'd do it myself if I could afford it."

She snapped a towel playfully at me and said, "Harrison Black, you aren't half as charming as you think you are."

I returned her smile. "Hey, if I'm halfway there, I'm still doing pretty well."

Millie frowned, then said, "Do you happen to know when Pearly's getting back?"

"Why, is something wrong around here? You know I'm pretty good with a tool belt myself."

She sighed. "No, nothing's in need of repair, but I do miss him."

"We all do," I said. I considered sharing Morton's dim view of our favorite handyman with her, but decided against it.

Speak of the devil and he appears, the old saying goes, but I hadn't said anything aloud about Morton, just focused on him briefly in my thoughts, and yet there he was, walking into the café like he was a man on a mission.

Unfortunately, I suspected I knew just what that mission was.

Fourteen

"I'M going to ask you one more time. Where is he, Harrison?"

"I told you, I don't know where Pearly is. We are talking about my handyman, aren't we?"

Morton scowled at me, then said, "You know it. I can't believe you'd flat-out lie to me."

I let my voice get loud enough to match his. "And I can't believe you're accusing me of it."

Millie joined us and said in a calmer voice, "Would you two like to take this shouting match outside? I've got customers who are trying to have a peaceful lunch."

I looked around and noticed that most folks eating at The Crocked Pot weren't even pretending to look away. When our gazes met, though, they dropped their chins and stared at their plates, but I knew they were still listening.

"She's right," I said. "Let's take this outside."

Morton turned on his heel and stalked out of the café. Millie asked, "What's he talking about, Harrison?"

"I wish I knew," I said. "You haven't seen Pearly around, have you?"

"No, I haven't seen him since he left."

"I haven't either, so why does he keep harassing me about it?"

The sheriff was outside waiting impatiently for me, his arms crossed over his chest.

I cut him off before he had the chance to say a word. "Listen, I don't know where you're getting your information, but Pearly's not here."

He snapped, "So I won't need a warrant to search your apartment?"

"Be my guest. Come on up, I'll show you around myself."

He followed me upstairs, and as we climbed the steps, I said, "I swear to you, I don't know where he is."

Morton just grunted. I unlocked my apartment door and he brushed past me. "You normally leave tools laying around on the furniture?" he said as looked down at the hammer perched on the end table by the entry.

I'd been using it to hang pictures and had forgotten to return it to Pearly's workbench. "Absolutely. There's a chainsaw on the bed, and I've got a router sitting in my bathtub."

He ignored my jibe and started looking around. It didn't take him long to search the apartment, it wasn't that big a space. The only place he even hesitated at was the ladder-bars in my closet that led up to the roof. "What's that?"

I wasn't all that excited about sharing the place with him, but I didn't have much choice. "It's the roof access. It's there for maintenance."

"Let's go," he said.

I started out of the closet when he called me back. "Not out there. We're going up."

I shook my head, but led him up the rungs to the roof. It had been my sanctuary, my peace in the world, and the sheriff was violating it. I'd considered telling him it was off-limits, but doing that would only make him that much more determined to go up there. There was a chance once he saw Pearly wasn't up there, he'd drop his crazy notion that I was hiding him.

I climbed up ahead of him and undid the hatch. After I stepped out onto the flat roof, Morton was there two seconds behind me. His gaze took in my storage bin, but since it was too small to hide Pearly, he didn't say anything about it.

"Listen, I'd appreciate it if you'd keep this to yourself. I come up here sometimes when I want to get away from the world."

He looked at me and shook his head. "Who am I going to tell?"

I followed him around the perimeter of the rooftop, but neither one of us said another word until we ended back up at the scuttle.

"It's like I told you; he's not here."

"This is a big building, Harrison. There are lots of places to hide."

"Sheriff, why would he run from you? You're not going to arrest him, are you?"

"If I could get my hands on him, I might. That newspaper article has brought me nothing but grief." I couldn't imagine the kind of pressure being applied on him. *The Gunpowder Gazette* had burned him at the stake for letting Pearly get away. It made what they'd done to me look like a love fest.

"I know it looks bad, but Pearly didn't kill her."

He waited until we were back in my apartment before he said, "If he's so innocent, then why is he hiding?"

"As far as I know, he's still in the mountains. What makes you think he's anywhere near River's Edge?"

Morton stormed out of my apartment and said, "I got a report he was spotted out here last night from a reliable source. He hasn't gone far, you can believe that."

"Have you checked his place? Most likely he doesn't know you're looking for him. You can't accuse Pearly of avoiding you if he's not aware you're after him."

Morton said, "We're keeping an eye on his house, but he's too smart to go back there. Besides, there are a lot more places to hide here, and he's been working this complex since Belle took over. Don't worry, I'll find him."

We walked back down the stairs, and I was surprised the sheriff hadn't insisted on checking out the other offices while we'd been up there. Markum had a nice space, as did Gary Cragg and a few other folks.

My answer came when we went outside.

There were three squad cars parked in front of River's Edge. It looked like it was going to be a thorough search after all.

I looked at the patrolmen and said, "You know, I'm not so sure this is a good idea."

Morton said, "So you have something to hide?"

"No, but I don't want you scaring my tenants or their customers. You're going to have to get that warrant after all."

Morton smiled, then reached out his hand to one of his female officers. She put a folded piece of paper in his grasp, and after Morton glanced at it, he handed it to me. It was a search warrant allowing him to look around the entire complex.

"If you had one of these, why did you bother asking my permission?"

"I had to keep you busy until the warrant got here so you couldn't warn Pearly first."

"He's not here," I insisted.

"And I say he is." Morton turned to his staff and said, "I've already checked the one apartment upstairs, but there are offices up there, too. You two check them out." He turned to the other two officers and said, "You'all start down by the pottery and I'll start at the candleshop at this end. Remember, he's wanted for questioning at the moment, and that's all. No rough stuff. Now go."

As his team dispersed, I followed him into my candleshop.

"I don't need a chaperone," he said.

"You do if you're going into At Wick's End."

He didn't like it, but he knew there wasn't anything he could do about it. Eve looked startled when the sheriff walked in behind me. "Harrison, what is it?" she asked, ignoring her customer for the moment.

"He thinks Pearly's here."

"And you let him storm in without resistance?"

"Eve, he's got a warrant, so there's really nothing I can do about it."

After the sheriff looked around, including the classroom, the storage area and our small bathroom, he said, "Okay, I'm going next door."

I followed him to the door, and he said, "I can't stop you from being in your candleshop, but you're not going with me everywhere on the grounds."

"I own this place, along with the bank. I can go wherever I please."

Morton snorted. "And I can haul you in for obstruction of justice."

That was about all I was willing to take. "I'd like to see you try it. I'm not a big fan of Gary Cragg, but I know you two like each other even less. I've got a feeling he'd love for you to try to keep me away."

"Do what you want," Morton snapped.

We walked into Heather's shop, The New Age. She was reading something at the register, and she nearly dropped the book when we walked in.

"I know this isn't a social call," she said, "not with all those patrol cars out front. What is this, a raid? If you're looking for contraband, all I've got are some rocks from Sri Lanka, but they were imported before the ban."

Morton said, "I'm looking for Pearly Gray."

Heather shook her head. "What's the matter, is it too dangerous looking for real criminals? He didn't do anything, and you know it."

"Then why is he on the run?" Morton said as he pushed through a beaded divider between Heather's shop and her backroom. Suddenly he said, "Why is this back door open? Was he just here?"

Heather stepped past him and closed it. "The latch isn't working, and I can't call Pearly to fix it, now can I?"

Morton worked the lock, tested the door, then said, "It looks okay to me."

"What can I say? Sometimes it works, sometimes it doesn't."

I turned to Heather and said, "I'll take a look at it myself after the sheriff is gone."

Heather nodded as Morton and I exited without another word.

Ultimately the three search parties wound up in front of Millie's place.

"Are you satisfied now that he's not here, Sheriff?"

Morton said, "Blast it all, I should have had a man in the alley. Don't worry, we'll get him." He paused, then said, "If he does turn up here, Harrison, I expect you to call me. At once."

"I'll be glad to if I see him."

After the sheriff and his staff were gone, I wondered just who had given him the tip that Pearly was at River's Edge. If my handyman was hanging around, he knew how to hide. I'd been all over the building in the last few days, and I hadn't seen a trace of him. I grabbed the tool belt from Pearly's storage area and went back to Heather's to fix that lock before someone took advantage of it.

"I thought he'd never leave," she said.

"Yeah, he's convinced Pearly's here."

"Why are you back, Harrison? Don't you have a shop to run?"

"Eve's got it covered," I said as I pulled out a Phillips head screwdriver. "I'm here to work on that latch."

"I tightened it myself. It should hold just fine until Pearly comes back."

I shrugged. "I just hope he decides to."

"Harrison Black, you can't honestly believe he killed that woman."

"Of course I don't," I said. "You have to admit, though, it doesn't look good, him staying on the run like this." While I was fairly certain my friend hadn't killed Gretel, Pearly had managed to completely hide his affair with the woman from me. What else was there about him that I didn't know? And what exactly was he capable of if his back was against the wall?

Heather said, "I'm sure he has his reasons. Good-bye, Harrison."

"See you later," I said as I walked back to the candle-shop. Heather and Pearly had always been close, but she should have known she didn't have to defend him to me. I wanted to believe just as much as she did that our handyman and friend hadn't shot Gretel Barnett. I was beginning to have a sneaking suspicion who did, but it wasn't enough. If Morton had been just a little more receptive to my input, I would have mentioned the clown Evelyn had seen at the celebration, for whatever amount of good it would have done. The whole thing was getting pretty complicated, and I didn't have a clue who to trust, or how far.

I knew one thing, though. Clown makeup was a perfect disguise that day, and there was no doubt in my mind that the killer would easily blend back into the festival's scenery after shooting Gretel. But who could the clown have been? I took the tool belt and put it back in Pearly's workroom. My foot kicked something as I laid the belt back on the workbench. I had to get a yardstick out to retrieve it as it skittered under the workbench. It was a tube of greasepaint with the logo from Party World on it.

Just like something a clown would wear.

The PW logo was tough to spot, faint silver print inscribed on the silver case, and I wondered if the murderer had even noticed it. The police would have, though; I was sure of that. I was just glad I'd found it and not the sheriff. If I'd told Morton about the sighting before he'd searched the building, that tube would be a strong piece of evidence against Pearly. Was it possible that someone was setting him up? Evelyn had been emphatic about seeing the clown, and that could be pretty damning testimony. Or was she lying, trying to frame Pearly?

I grabbed an empty jar and nudged the tube into it, then sealed the lid. If there were fingerprints on it, I didn't want to disturb them any more than I had. More importantly, I wanted to get that tube out of River's Edge before Morton found a way to tie it to what had happened at the festival. I searched the workroom as best I could, but I couldn't find anything else that could be construed as evidence against Pearly. I decided to stash what I'd found with April May until I could figure out who was out to frame my handyman. The possibility that he'd left it there himself was one I wasn't willing to consider at the moment.

I was nearly at A Slice of Heaven before I realized I hadn't told Eve where I was going. I'd have to make it a quick trip before she walked out on me in protest of my increasing absences from the candleshop. Though my assistant and my handyman had gone through some personal problems in the past, I was willing to bet she didn't believe him capable of killing either.

I took the jar off the truck seat beside me and wrapped it in a worn T-shirt I kept under the seat to use as a rag when I washed one of my pickups.

It was between the lunch and dinner rushes, and I found April studying the selections on the jukebox. "Harrison Black, it's good to see you out in the world again."

"It's good to be here," I said. "April, I need a favor. No questions asked."

"Name it," she said.

"It's going to be that easy?"

April grinned. "You just told me I couldn't ask about it. Besides, if I push you on it now, you're going to have to come up with a lie, and I don't believe in lying between friends."

"You're one of a kind," I said.

"And more of the world should take notice of it," she said. "Now what can I do for you?"

"I need you to hide this for me."

She took the covered jar, then said, "Is it dangerous? Will it bite, explode or leak?"

"No, if you look at it that way, it's perfectly safe."

She nodded. "But it's dangerous nonetheless, gotcha. Consider it in safe hands."

I hugged her, and as I pulled back, I saw April blush slightly. "Thanks," I said, "I do appreciate it."

"Not a problem. I would like to ask you for a favor myself. Don't worry, I'll hide this no matter what your answer is."

"What is it?"

"When this is all over, will you tell me what I've been hiding?"

"I promise."

As I drove back to River's Edge, I felt a wash of relief getting that makeup out of the complex. Now I needed to find out who had placed it there, and why they were so eager to set my friend up.

I decided to stop off at Party World on my way back to the candleshop. Eve wouldn't be happy about the delay, but I had to find out how tough that greasepaint was to buy. I was hoping that maybe, just maybe, the killer had slipped up somehow.

"I'm looking for some greasepaint, the kind that clowns wear," I asked the clerk at Party World. The building, full of costumes, balloons, plates, cups and everything else needed for a celebration, was laid out like a maze, and I hadn't had any luck after searching the aisles for ten minutes. I'd finally found a teenaged employee who was more interested in making time with the female clerk beside him than helping me. Only by standing directly between them did I finally manage to get his attention.

"Aisle 7, next to the fright wigs," he reluctantly admitted.

"Thanks, you've been a great help."

"No problem," he said, missing my sarcasm completely and turning his attention back to his comely coworker. I hated that expression more than his behavior. When did "no problem" enter the common vernacular, and where had I been when they'd taken the vote? It was dismissive and disrespectful, and I didn't care for it.

I headed off to the fright wigs and clown makeup, hoping that the tube I'd held was a special-order item, something they could trace.

There were three dozen tubes on the shelf just like the one I'd found under Pearly's workbench. So much for following that lead. It was time to head back to the candleshop. No doubt Eve was ready to put out an all-points bulletin on me, I'd been gone so long.

I got back to the shop, ready with a dozen apologies for my employee, but one look at her face told me that something bigger than my absenteeism was going on.

She said, "Thank goodness you're here. You need to get to the hospital as quickly as you can. Your friend Becka's been attacked."

Fifteen

"WHAT happened to her?" I asked.

"She was jogging by the river near here and some maniac mugged her. She tumbled down the bank and fell into the water."

"Is it serious?"

Eve said, "They wouldn't say, but she's been asking for you. Go, Harrison, I can stay here as long as you need me to."

I tore off toward the hospital, fighting to keep myself from driving too far over the speed limit. Wrecking on the way over there wasn't going to do either one of us any good.

I found the nurses' station and was directed to Becka's room. It was semiprivate, so at least she wasn't in Intensive Care. One side of her face was scraped, and her right arm was in a cast. Her room was an explosion of color and scent; someone had already gone out of their way to make her feel cared for.

"Hey there. Are you okay?"

She nodded as she offered me a slight smile. "I think so. They just gave me something for the pain. I don't feel like there's really any reason for me to stay here overnight, but they want to keep an eye on me. Evidently I blacked out at some point."

"So what happened?" I asked as I stood beside her bed.

"It was the craziest thing. I was jogging by the Gunpowder like I always do, when somebody came out of nowhere, shoved me, and I twisted my ankle and fell. I had my headphones on. I didn't even hear them coming up behind me. The next thing I knew I was being pulled out of the river." She rubbed her scalp with her free hand and added, "They tell me it's not unusual to forget parts of what happened when there's a head injury."

Trying to lighten the mood, I pointed to the flowers and said, "What's all this? I didn't know you had so many admirers."

She looked troubled. "They were just delivered a few minutes ago. You mean they're not from you?"

"Becka, we're just friends. This is a little extravagant for my budget even if we were engaged." Becka and I had had a rocky time together, and there was no way I'd ever date her again, though I was happy to be her friend. There was just always too much pressure when I was in a relationship with her. Nothing was ever good enough, and I never lived up to my potential, at least as far as she was concerned.

She looked crestfallen. "I just thought . . . you know . . ."

I pulled out the card on the closest arrangement and asked, "Is it okay if I read this?"

"Go right ahead," she said.

The card was inscribed, *From someone who loves you.* I said, "So you really don't know who this is from."

"Not a clue. Like I said, I was kind of hoping it was you."

I reached for the telephone, then dialed the number of the florist on the card. After a brief conversation, I hung up and explained, "They said it was a cash transaction from a messenger service. No way to trace it, I'm afraid."

Her eyes widened. "Do you think they're from him? Why would he try to kill me, and then shower me with flowers?"

"Who are you talking about?"

Urgently, she said, "My stalker. I know they're from him. Get them out of here, Harrison, they're creeping me out."

"Take it easy," I said. "We don't know they're from him."

"Who else would send them? Get rid of them. Now." Her voice was loud and shrill. At least there was no one sharing her room at the moment.

A nurse popped her head in. "Is there a problem here?"

With as much dignity as I could muster, I said, "The lady has decided she doesn't care for the flowers."

The woman said, "Man, I'd love to get this kind of attention. Are you sure?"

Becka said, "You can have them."

"I can't, it's against hospital policy."

"Then throw them out. I don't want them." There was no way to misinterpret her resolve. The nurse shrugged, then said, "Okay, I'll find something to do with them."

I helped her carry the bouquets out of the room, telling Becka I'd be right back. As I walked to one of the nurses' stations, the woman said, "She seemed so happy to get them before. What's the matter, did you two have a fight?"

I wasn't about to correct her. "They're not from me."

The nurse nodded knowingly. "From another guy, huh? So you're making her throw them out."

"I'm not making her do anything," I said. "And if you knew Becka Lane at all, you'd realize that."

After we'd collected all the flowers and removed them, I said, "It looks kind of bare in here now, doesn't it?"

Becka said, "I prefer it to having those things around me."

I moved to a chair near her bed and asked, "So you don't have any idea who was behind you?"

"I felt a shove between my shoulder blades, then I twisted my ankle and I fell. That's all I know."

She was getting hysterical. I patted her hand and said, "Listen, you're okay now. That's all that counts."

"Harrison, I'm getting scared, really scared, now."

"We can call the sheriff again," I said. "This is a little more concrete than what we've had before."

"Oh please, he's not going to give this any credence. I don't need that."

"Don't worry," I said. "I'll talk to him myself."

"I wish you wouldn't. It's not going to do any good."

"I think you're wrong," I pressed. "He needs to know what happened."

"Fine, tell him anything you want then. Harrison, I think the pain medication is kicking in. Thanks for coming by, but I really don't feel up to talking right now."

"I'll come back later," I said, "with flowers of my own next time."

She shivered, despite the blanket pulled up around her. "Thank you for the thought, but I'd rather have balloons or some magazines. Anything but flowers. Ugh."

"No flowers," I promised and left her room. As I walked toward the elevator, I noticed that one of the arrangements Becka had discarded was sitting at the nurses' station. I wasn't sure how she'd react when she saw that. I also wasn't all that sure I wanted to replace the offerings she'd gotten with anything else. It occurred to me that Becka was using the stalking incidents to get closer to me, and I honestly wasn't interested in reopening that relationship with her. Even if I didn't have my hands full with the candleshop and the entire River's Edge complex, Becka and I had broken up for some very good reasons, and none of them had changed.

It was time to stop being her guardian and turn the job over to the police.

I bumped into Vince in the lobby, a vase of flowers in his hand. I said, "If I were you, I'd swap those out for a stuffed animal or something."

Vince said, "Why, did you already give her flowers?"

"Me? No way, but somebody did, and she thinks they're from the guy who was stalking her."

Vince shook his head. "This guy just doesn't give up, does he? What do the cops have to say about it?"

"She doesn't want to call them. I tried to convince her they needed to know, but she won't listen to me. Maybe you'll have more luck than I did."

He shrugged. "I don't know, Becka kind of has a mind of her own."

"You don't have to tell me that; we dated, remember? Vince, don't let her go back to her apartment. Make her go to her sister's place if you can. She's got to stop being a target or something a whole lot worse may happen to her."

"I'll try."

I felt better with Vince there watching over her. I just hoped he'd have more luck with her than I had.

Back at the candleshop, I found Eve waiting on a pair of customers in the sheet wax section. She nodded toward me, but I wanted to wait until our customers were gone before I brought up all that had happened. After Eve rang up the sales, she said, "How's Becka doing?"

"She scraped her face and broke one arm. Other than that, she's going to be fine. She had quite a scare, though. Somebody shoved her from behind, and she tumbled into the river."

"Did they find out who pushed her?"

"That's the thing. Nobody else was around." I decided to keep my suspicions to myself about Becka's renewed interest in me. I was sure Eve would have something to say, most likely a crack I didn't need to hear.

I followed Eve to our office, and she grabbed her sweater off the hook on the door. "Well, you've certainly had quite a day, haven't you?"

"I'm sorry I wasn't here to help you with the shop. I've been an absentee owner lately."

She shrugged. "Don't worry about it, you'll have plenty of time to work this evening. You do remember you're closing by yourself tonight, right?" We'd worked out a new schedule that reduced Eve's hours until we could get back on our feet again. Naturally I'd forgotten all about it rushing around Micah's Ridge.

"Absolutely. Have a nice evening."

"You, too," she said. "See you tomorrow afternoon, Harrison."

"Good night." After she was gone, I ran a report to see what kind of day she'd had without me. The numbers were better than I had any right to expect. Maybe folks were starting to forget that scathing article in the newspaper about me. It was amazing how much dirt they'd thrown at me based on one hysterical woman's delusions. I guessed it all depended on who the hysterical woman was, or more importantly in this case, who she was married to.

I GOT A phone call as I was helping a customer with a candlemaking kit for her mother's birthday. I hated to answer the telephone when I was with someone, because I figured if a customer took the trouble to come to the shop, they deserved preferential treatment over someone who just called.

"At Wick's End, can you hold, please?"

"Harrison, it's Jubal Grant at the candleshop. Call me when you get free."

"Good enough," I said and hung up. After the sale, I returned Jubal's call.

"Sorry about that," I said. "I was with a customer."

"I applaud you for putting them first," Jubal said. "Working retail is certainly more taxing than I thought it would be."

"I know exactly what you mean. I think everybody should have to spend a month of their lives waiting on other people. I don't care if they sell clothes, candles or wait tables; I bet it would improve most folks' manners."

"No doubt. I was calling about Pearly. That was a rather scathing hatchet job the newspaper did, wasn't it?"

"They did everything but flat-out accuse him of shooting her," I agreed.

"Has he been arrested?"

"No, the sheriff doesn't have enough on him yet, but he is looking pretty hard for him."

"You mean he's gone?"

I took the chance to straighten the displays on the counter as we talked. "He took some long-due vacation time. Losing your cousin was quite a blow to him."

"Of course, I understand."

I couldn't let him think that Pearly was a murderer. "I know how thorough a job the newspaper did hanging this on him, but I promise you, Pearly didn't kill Gretel any more than I did."

Jubal paused, then said, "I wish I could be as certain as you are. They left things rather badly between them."

"I've got me eye on someone else," I said rashly. I didn't really, but I couldn't let Jubal think Pearly could have done such a cold-blooded thing. I nodded to a customer who walked in and told Jubal, "Listen, I've got to go."

"Whom do you suspect?" Jubal asked.

I'd been holding the phone against my cheek and shoulder as I'd been straightening things up, and before I could answer him, it slipped out of my grip. By the time I grabbed it to explain, he was already gone.

I'd have to call him back later and tell him I hadn't just hung up on him, but at the moment I had a customer to wait on. It didn't do either of us any good to speculate further about what was going to happen to Pearly. I was frankly glad for the distraction my customers brought me. In the end, I'd much rather focus on candlemaking than crime, no matter how worried I was about my friend.

I SOLD SEVERAL blocks of wax, some dyes and scents and a pair of nice beginning candlemaking kits as the evening progressed. It was ten minutes until closing time, and I was happy to be back in my element surrounded by all those candles and supplies.

Then the chime over the door announced another visitor. It wasn't another customer, though. Markum walked in and said abruptly, "Close up early, Harrison. There's something you need to see."

"What is it? You have no idea how cranky Eve gets when I lock the doors before I'm supposed to."

Markum looked around. "Is she here?"

"No, she left at five."

He shrugged. "So she'll never know."

"Believe me, she'll know. I don't know how, but I'd swear she has a spy around here to keep tabs on me when she's gone."

"Harrison, do you own this place or does she?"

I smiled. "Technically, most of it belongs to the bank. From the way I figure it, I own the bay window up front and part of one aisle."

"This is important," he said.

"Okay, I believe you." I flipped the sign from OPEN to CLOSED and deadbolted the door. "Where are we going?" I asked. "Do I need my truck keys?"

Instead of answering, he pointed to Heather's shop. I looked in and saw that the lights were still on, and caught a quick glimpse of Heather as she moved around in the back of her store sweeping the floor.

"So? You brought me out here to see Heather working?"

He shook his head, then tapped the door gently to draw my attention to the print, but not loud enough to alert Heather that we were outside. "Look at the hours," Markum said.

I studied the listing, then said, "Okay, so she's staying open past her regular business hours. I do that myself now and then."

Markum stepped up and opened the door. "Let's go in and see, shall we?"

When Heather saw us, she said, "Hey, what are two

doing here this late? Do we have a community watch program I didn't know about?"

Markum ignored the jibe. "You're not supposed to be open tonight. In fact, you were here late last night too."

Heather stopped sweeping. "Are you keeping tabs on me now, Markum?"

"It's just curious behavior," he said.

Heather started sweeping again at a faster pace. "If you must know, business is down. I figure the more hours I can keep the shop open, the better chance I have of making my nut and start bringing in some profits."

Markum said softly, "It's a nice story." In a louder voice, he said, "Come on out, Pearly, I know you're back there."

Heather said, "Have you lost your mind?"

As she said it, there was the sound of a box falling in the backroom. Markum said, "And I suppose that's just your resident ghost."

"Esmeralda's probably chasing her shadow back there again."

I spotted the cat curled up on a shelf near me. As I reached down, she jumped up in my arms. "It's a good trick if she's doing it. Heather, what's going on here? Is Pearly hiding in your shop?"

She said, "Now don't you start, Harrison."

At that moment, Pearly Gray walked out of the backroom and joined us. "Thanks for trying, Heather, but they had to find out sooner or later."

It was hard to tell who she was angrier with, Markum and me for exposing her, or Pearly for revealing himself. She huffed once, then put the broom down. "At least I can stop sweeping as a pretense for being here. I've just about worn a hole in the floor."

"When did you get back, Pearly?" I asked.

Markum stepped up and added, "More importantly, why are you hiding in here like you're guilty of something?"

Pearly snapped, "You've seen the paper. They did a rather thorough character assassination, wouldn't you say? I was surprised there was no implication that I'd finally stopped beating my wife."

Heather said, "You're not married anymore, Pearly."

"It's a figure of speech, my dear." He turned back to us and said, "I got wind of the article before it was published, so I decided to come back to River's Edge, where I could keep my eye on what was happening without being under the scrutiny of the police."

"There's something you two should know," I said. "I would have kept your secret."

"So would I," Markum said.

"Gentlemen, it was not my intent to exclude either one of you. Heather happened to catch me in my workroom the night I got back. I'm afraid I was rather careless there. I forgot to lock the door behind me."

"I had to borrow a screwdriver to fix my back door," Heather said. "I knew in a heartbeat that Pearly couldn't stay in his shop; that's the first place Morton would look for him. I gave him a key to my place, and I've been smuggling food to him since then."

That explained the double orders Heather had been making with Millie. I doubted it would have escaped the café owner's attention, but Millie was an expert at keeping her suspicions to herself if the situation merited it.

"So have you had any luck in your investigation?" I asked Pearly.

"Alas, no. If I could move around without fear of imprisonment, perhaps I'd be able to uncover something, but it's difficult investigating when I'm under suspicion myself."

"Tell me about it," I said.

Markum looked at me, and I shrugged. He took it as my approval and said, "Harrison and I are looking into Gretel's murder ourselves." I suddenly realized I hadn't shared my discovery of the tube of greasepaint with Markum yet.

A ray of hope shined behind Pearly's eyes. "Gentlemen, I can't tell you how much I appreciate that. Have you had any success yet?"

I tried to sound reassuring as I said, "We've got some leads we're tracking down, but it's taking longer than I'd like."

Pearly said, "I'll hide as long as I have to."

The night outside was suddenly interrupted by flashing red-and-blue lights. Pearly said in a voice full of sadness, "They've found me."

I snapped, "Go into the storeroom. Don't leave unless you hear me coughing. That means they're getting closer."

"Why not just flee out the back?" Pearly asked.

"They'll be watching the rear entrance," Markum said. "Harrison's right. Don't take off until you have to."

He disappeared in back and was gone twenty seconds before a uniformed police woman came in. At least we were having some luck. Nobody would be as tenacious as the sheriff in his search for Pearly.

Heather asked the cop, "Can I help you?"

"I'm looking for your handyman, Pearly Gray," the woman said.

I glanced at her nameplate and saw her name was Kelner. "Officer Kelner, I've already told your boss, I don't know where Pearly is." Technically it was the truth. Sure, he was somewhere lurking in the backroom, but I didn't know his exact location.

She looked around, then said, "There were four of you in here when I drove up."

I held Esme up. "There are four of us here now."

She shook her head. "That's not what I mean, and you know it." She started for the backroom, and I was just about to cough to warn Pearly when Kelner's radio on her belt went off. "Toni, where are you?"

"I'm at the hippie shop at River's Edge," she answered.

"It's called The New Age," Heather said stiffly, but it was lost on the cop.

"Well, get over to Mulberry and Main. Some lunatic just drove into Ridgway Flowers."

"I'm on my way," she said, forgetting all about her suspicions.

After I was certain she was gone, I called out, "Pearly, you can come out now. She just left."

Silence.

"Come on, it's all right."

The three of us walked into the backroom. The first thing I saw was the exit door, standing wide open. It looked like Pearly had decided to run after all.

Sixteen

WE waited around Heather's shop for an hour, hoping that Pearly would come back, but we finally realized it was a lost cause.

Markum said, "I've got some calls to make, but if he shows up again, call me, Heather."

She said, "Do you honestly think he's coming back after that? He probably thinks we called the police ourselves."

"Come on, you know he doesn't think that at all. Pearly knows he can trust us. Markum's right, though. There's no sense in us hanging around here."

"You two go on, then. I'm staying."

Markum said, "Suit yourself. Harrison, I'll be upstairs in my office for another twenty minutes, then I'm going to my place. If you need me, call me there, okay?"

"I'll do it. Thanks."

After Markum was gone, I said, "Are you sure it's a good idea to just hang around here?"

"I've got nowhere else I need to be," Heather said.

"Think about it. If your still here when that cop comes back, she's going to want to look around. Why don't we get out of here, turn out the lights and give Pearly a chance to come back without being seen?"

After a moment's thought, Heather said, "You're right. I don't know why I'm so worried about him. He's old enough to be my father. He can take care of himself."

"It's okay," I said, "You worry because you're a good friend."

I walked Heather out as she locked up her shop. Then she turned to me and said, "Would you like to grab some dinner? We could go over to A Slice of Heaven."

"Thanks, but I've got to run my reports, make out my deposit, restock shelves and get an order ready for tomorrow. I'm going to be here for a while."

"Okay, but I'll give you a rain check," she said.

"And I'll cash it once things slow down around here," I said.

I walked back to the candleshop, wishing I'd brought a jacket with me. Even though I was wearing one of my favorite flannel shirts, the wind was biting enough to make me wish I had more on. There wouldn't be any rooftop soirées tonight.

The total on my report was healthy enough to make me believe that the worst of our slump was over. Steadily our business had been picking up until we were nearly at the levels we'd been at before Gretel had died. I had half-expected another slow period when Pearly had been named as a suspect. After all, the paper had gone out of its way to tie him to River's Edge in their story. Though some of my other tenants might have seen some fluctuations because of it, it hadn't affected me, at least not yet.

I did my chores, locked the shop and considered leav-

ing the deposit for the next day. But if I did that, I knew I'd
have to tell Eve I'd skipped a day at the bank, and frankly,
it wasn't worth it. Besides, though it was chilly out, it was
a beautiful night for the short drive into town. I was
sleepier than I'd realized, though, and the warm air from
the heater was lulling me into a rest I couldn't afford to
take yet. I shut the blower off and rolled both windows
down, letting the cold air wash over me as I drove. There
was no danger of me falling asleep after that.

By the time I got back to my apartment, I was ready
for a quick sandwich and then bed. It was hard enough
standing up working all day at the candleshop, but running around grilling people without letting them know
why was even more of a strain. I was ready for some
sleep, and hopefully I'd be rested up enough the next day
to keep tracking down the person who had shot Gretel
Barnett.

A GHASTLY CRYING clown was chasing me in my sleep
when I jolted suddenly awake.

An explosion still echoed outside as I jumped out of
bed. It sounded as if a car had blown up in the parking
lot. I reached for the aluminum baseball bat I kept by the
door for emergencies, but it wasn't there. Then I remembered I'd loaned it to Suzanne for a church league game.
Not wanting to go outside without some kind of protection, I grabbed the hammer on the end table by the door,
and was glad I'd forgotten to return it to its proper place.
I raced out of my apartment and flipped on the light to the
stairs. Nothing happened. There was something wrong
with the switch or the fixture; Pearly had just replaced the
bulb two weeks ago. Barely pausing, I hit the first step,

then I felt my feet go out from under me as I missed the second one.

THE CLAW ON the other end of the hammer saved me. Without thinking, I threw my hands out to stop my fall, and luckily, the clawed end dug into the drywall, acting as an anchor. Pearly would have a sizable hole to patch and I'd have a sore tailbone for a while, but that beat tumbling down the long flight of stairs. I crawled back up to the landing, managed to pull myself to a standing position, then limped back to my apartment for a flashlight. I found it, then studied the step where I'd tripped.

A handful of children's marbles were scattered on the second step, as well as a few below it. It was no wonder I'd fallen.

Carefully holding the rail, I brushed the marbles aside and went outside to see what had happened. One of the trashcans I kept on the walkway was in the middle of the parking lot, far enough away from the automatic lights to keep from tripping the switch. The can was smoking, and from the heavy smell of gunpowder in the air, I knew someone had lit an M-80 firecracker. They were supposed to be illegal in North Carolina, but there were places across the border in South Carolina they could be had, for a price.

It was clear someone had used the trashcan as a ruse to get me downstairs in a hurry so I could break my neck on the steps. But who would want me dead, or hurt enough so that I would be out of the picture?

I pulled the trashcan back in its place and realized that the lights never came on. Had they been disabled as well? No, when I walked back to the stairwell door, the lights came on. So there was a dead spot in our layout. Had the attacker known that, or had he just been lucky? I didn't want to think about the first option, since Pearly and I had installed those lights ourselves.

I collected the marbles and headed back upstairs. I decided to keep the incident to myself in case I could use the information later. Fortunately, it hadn't turned out as the culprit had hoped, so only two of us knew about the marbles. After taking a couple of Tylenols, I stretched out on the couch with a book, knowing that sleep was most likely out of the question. To my great surprise, I woke up the next morning with a sore rear end and a burning curiosity about who had tried to kill me the night before.

I WAS GETTING ready to open the candleshop when there was a persistent knocking at the front door. I tried to ignore it, since I still needed to do a few things before we opened and I was moving a little slower than usual, but the pounding was relentless.

"We're not open yet," I said as I walked to the front of the shop.

Jubal looked startled to see me as I opened the door for him. "Good, I'm glad I caught you in. I'm so sorry to bother you," he said. "I just need a minute of your time."

I unlocked the door and stepped aside. "Come on in, Jubal. I thought it was just another overenthusiastic candlemaker."

He tried to smile, and almost made it. "Do you get many of those?"

"We have our share. What can I do for you? Wait a second, it's about what happened yesterday, isn't it? Sorry I never got back to you. I didn't hang up on you. The phone slipped off my shoulder, and by the time I retrieved it, I got overwhelmed with customers and forgot all about our conversation."

"Please, there's no need to explain. I must admit, you left me curious with that cryptic comment of yours. Are you truly close to something?"

I admitted, "I'm beginning to think it was wishful thinking. Sorry about that. I didn't mean to get your hopes up."

Jubal didn't look upset at all. "It's no problem, really. We both just want to know what really happened to Gretel."

"So if you're not here for an apology, what brings you out to River's Edge?"

"I wanted you to know Flickering Lights is shutting down."

Though I couldn't say the news of my chief competition closing upset me, I did feel bad for Jubal. "How did that happen?"

"They finally managed to track Hans down, and he wants the shop closed as soon as possible. He's even letting the franchise revert, but since Gretel paid in full for an exclusivity clause, the candle shop won't be back to haunt you later. Evidently I've been given free reign to liquidate any way I see fit. If you can imagine, he's not even coming to Micah's Ridge to handle the estate. There was something too pressing in South America that he couldn't leave, he told me." Jubal shook his head. "Hans never was all that concerned with details." He paused, then added, "I suppose I shouldn't complain. Since Gretel left me out of the list of beneficiaries, Hans is allowing me to keep the proceeds of the liquidation, as long as I do it quickly."

I'd been curious about that since Markum and I had uncovered the fact of his absence in Gretel's will, and this was the perfect time to satisfy my curiosity. "Why did she neglect you, do you suppose?"

Jubal said, "Don't look so surprised, Harrison, I knew Gretel's intent, and heartily endorsed it. Ten years ago I found myself in a predicament, one that required an immediate and generous cash transfusion. I never would have asked Gretel for help, but she got wind of it and bailed me out. That's one of the reasons I came down to be with her, actually. I never thanked her as well as I should have."

"I'm sure she knew you were grateful," I said, happy to have at least that point solved.

Jubal said, "The reason I'm here is that I was wondering if you might be interested in buying my supplies. In fact, I can make you a good deal, less than wholesale, if you take the entire inventory off my hands immediately."

"I should tell you that you'd make more if you took a few weeks and had a 'Going Out of Business' sale. I'm not sure if I could do better than what you'd make that way."

Jubal idly spun a ring on his left hand. "I appreciate your candor, but it appears I'm being forced to evacuate the premises in forty-eight hours. There's really no time to do it properly, and truth be told, as charming as your little town is, I can't say I'll be sorry to go. Bad memories and all that, you understand."

"Completely," I said. "How about this? I'll come by this evening and look over your stock. Then tomorrow I can get together with Eve and we'll have a figure for you by noon. I can't promise even fair market value, but I should be able to come up with something."

Jubal pumped my hand. "That's all I can ask. I appreciate your promptness in this. I'll see you this evening, then."

Heather was standing at the door when I let Jubal out.

She had Esme in her arms, and Jubal stepped a few paces back when he saw her. "I love cats, but unfortunately I'm allergic to them. It breaks my heart that I can't have one of my own."

Heather said, "I don't know what I'd do without Esmeralda, though I imagine Harrison would take her in a heartbeat if we ever had to split up."

"I guess she's okay as a temporary boarder, but I don't know about anything more permanent than that." If Esme was offended by the statement, she didn't show it.

Heather laughed. "Don't let him lie to you; he's a great deal fonder of this gal than he lets on."

Jubal said, "Well, I really must go. Until tonight, Harrison."

Heather walked into the candleshop and said, "Has Pearly been by your place?"

"No, I haven't seen him."

"Harrison, I'm really worried about him. He didn't sleep in the shop last night. In fact, he hasn't been back since that cop came by. He thinks I turned him in. I just know it." Esme started to squirm in her arms, but Heather held fast. It was pretty obvious the cat was picking up on her unsettled mood.

"Come on, Heather, he knows you better than that. If he didn't come back, it's probably because he knows River's Edge is the logical place for the sheriff to keep looking for him. Pearly's a brilliant man. He's not going to get caught in a trap."

"I hope you're right," she said. "I feel responsible for what happened."

"You didn't call the police, did you?"

"Of course not."

"Then you've got nothing to feel guilty about, Heather."

I glanced at my watch. "Shouldn't you be opening up? I know it's almost time for me to start my day."

Heather got it. "I'm sorry, Harrison, I didn't mean to keep you from your work."

I gave Esme a quick rub under the chin, put my hands on Heather's shoulders, then said, "Don't worry, about him. He's all right. Have faith in Pearly."

She nodded. "You're right. I'm probably just overreacting."

After she and her companion were gone, I saw that I only had two minutes before opening, so I switched the sign from CLOSED to OPEN and got ready to face another day's worth of customers.

I'd had a pretty decent morning when Mrs. Jorgenson came in, holding a set of small glass containers in her hand. "I've got a problem," she said as she thrust them out to me.

I took them and studied the first one. She had neatly arranged some semiprecious stones in the bottom of the container and had poured red-tinted wax around them. However, there were huge gaps between the rocks and the wax, and the gel wax itself was filled with so many bubbles it was hard to see what was suspended in it. I said, "The wax was too cool when you poured this one."

I studied the next one and saw that there were segments of wax in it, as if she'd waited for the wax to partially coalesce before pouring it. "You must have spooned the wax out for this one. You can always reheat it once it cools, you know."

She took the candles back from me. "No, I didn't realize that." After studying the candle with lumps in it, she said, "You know, I'm beginning to like this look. It's growing on me."

"It certainly has its own charm, doesn't it?"

She nodded. "More heat it is then. I confess I was interrupted during my session, and I neglected to recheck the temperature before I poured. Thank you, Harrison."

"You're most welcome. Would you like to try it again here? I can set you up in ten minutes, and I promise I won't let anyone distract you."

She shook her head. "No, I'd better get back home. I will make a sincere effort be more careful next time. Thank you. Just add this session to my bill."

I had to look twice to see if she was kidding, and I still couldn't tell. "Mrs. Jorgenson, this one's on the house."

"I don't take charity or handouts, Mr. Black. You should know that about me."

"My advice is free. I give it to anyone who walks in the door, and I never hand them a bill for it."

She frowned, then said, "I won't hear of it, and I expect that to be the final word on the subject."

"Fine, have it your way." If she insisted on paying for something I gave freely to anyone else who came into my shop, I'd find a way to give it back to her, either through a discount on her supplies or a few extras in her bag the next time she went on a shopping binge. There were some real benefits to owning the place myself, and if I couldn't hand out a free candle every now and then, I didn't want to be in business.

Seventeen

"I didn't know you came out in the daylight," I joked with Markum when he walked into the candleshop just before lunch. "I was beginning to wonder if you were a vampire or something."

Markum yawned, then covered it with his massive hand. "Yeah, this isn't exactly my time of day, but I've got to adjust to a new schedule."

"Is it the job in Eastern Europe you were telling me about?"

"No, it's something else," he said, picking up a carved candle I'd done a week earlier. "How do you get it to drip like this?"

"You have to do it while the wax is still warm," I said.

He glanced at the price, so I added, "It's a time-consuming process."

"Harrison, I run my own business, too, remember? You have to charge what the job is worth to you, or it doesn't make sense doing it." He pulled out his wallet and said, "In fact, I'd like this one for my office."

There were no customers in my shop at the time. "Tell you what, you can have it. You've helped me out enough out here."

Markum slid two twenties across the counter. "Appreciate the offer, but I think I'll enjoy it more if I pay for it."

I took his money, handed him a little change, and said, "Then I thank you."

He grinned. "Now I can burn it without any guilt. If you'd have given me the thing, I'd have felt bad every time I lit it." He said, "Pearly been around?"

"Heather was here this morning asking the same thing. If he's anywhere near River's Edge, he hasn't let me know about it. I told Heather he was a big boy. He's been taking care of himself long before any of us were around."

"Too true, but he hasn't had a cloud like this one hanging over him, I'll wager."

That got my attention. "Do you think we should be worried?"

He shook his head. "No, I'm sure he's fine. Knowing Pearly, he's probably got three or four places to hide out, no doubt rated in order by convenience, amenities and risks of being discovered. The man's methodical; you have to give him that."

Talking about Pearly, I suddenly realized I hadn't told Markum about what I'd discovered under the handyman's workbench or about Evelyn spotting the clown just before Gretel had been shot. "I've been meaning to tell you something. I uncovered two things that I think might be related to what happened to Gretel. I found a tube of greasepaint under Pearly's workbench yesterday, and a woman I saw at the festival just before Gretel was shot said she saw a clown hanging around Gretel's booth. It would be the perfect disguise with all that activity going on, wouldn't it? It sounds like somebody's trying to set Pearly up."

"It surely does. Did you see anybody dressed like a clown the day of the fair?"

There had been clowns, jugglers and balloon-twisters wandering the streets all morning, but then I remembered the clown perched on the courthouse steps. "You know what? I think I nearly tripped on him." I told Markum what I'd seen the day of the festival.

He said, "So at least now we think we know what happened. One of our suspects was dressed up like a clown, pulled out a gun and shot Gretel, then faded back into the crowd."

He paused, then added, "Harrison, I've just about decided that Runion was responsible for Gretel's murder. There's little doubt in my mind that he did it. I keep thinking about who had the most to gain, and he keeps coming up number one. I don't know how much he stood to make if he could buy Gretel's property, but you can bet it's more than the forty grand those masks Pearly got are worth. Even Hans's share would be peanuts compared to the total take Runion was set to bring in."

"I don't know, I keep thinking Hans had to have had something to do with her death. Don't forget, he had a lot to gain, too."

Markum said, "But what if Runion was sure Hans would sell the building if he inherited it from Gretel? Wouldn't that give him enough of a push to expedite the inheritance?"

"If that's true, wouldn't that mean that Hans would have to be around?" I said. "I'm starting to wonder if Pearly's the only one hiding around here. Think about it. We don't have anyone's word that he's out of town, except for Jubal. How hard is it to fake a long-distance telephone call, anyway? These days it's as easy to call from London as it is Charlotte."

Markum nodded. "You've got a point. Now I'm not generally a trusting soul, but why did I so readily accept the fact that man was out of the country? Harrison, my friend, perhaps it's time I went into another line of work. If my internal lie detector isn't working, I don't have a chance doing what I do."

"Don't be so hard on yourself," I said. "This isn't one of your business adventures."

"No, but it's turned out to be some kind of twisted hobby, hasn't it? So what's the complete list? Who do we think might have had a hand in this?"

I took a paper bag from under the counter, the type Belle had used before I took over. I'd switched over to plastic because it was cheaper to print our candlelit logo, but Eve preferred the old style, so we kept both at the register, at least until we ran out of the paper. "Let's list our suspects," I said. "First, there's Hans."

"I don't agree he's number one, at least not by himself," Markum said.

"This isn't in any particular order, but if it will make you feel better, we'll put Runion first." I squeezed Runion's name in on top of Hans's, then jotted down Martin Graybill's name.

"Who's this character?"

I explained to Markum, "He owns a restaurant on the block Runion wanted to buy. The man's pretty desperate to move out of town, and Gretel's refusal killed that dream."

"Okay, he can stay. Don't forget your Mrs. Jorgenson. She needs to be on that list, too."

"Come on, do you really think she could have done it? I don't believe it. If nothing else, I can't see her dressing up as a clown and shooting someone. You don't know her as well as I do. It would be beneath her."

Markum tapped the bag. "We're just hypothesizing here, remember? Besides, she could have paid someone to do it. Put her down."

I reluctantly wrote down "Mrs. J," then said, "Who else does that leave? There's an investor in Minnesota who owns part of that block, but from what I understand, he's never even been here. At least that's what Runion said. So where does that leave us?"

Markum studied the list, then said, "Well, I'm pretty sure Pearly didn't do it, and I think we can rule you out as well. You couldn't very well be in two places at once, dressed up as a clown and running your booth at the same time."

"Gee, thanks for your support," I said.

He smiled. "Come on, Harrison, I'm kidding. I don't think Jubal killed her; he didn't have any motive since she left him squat, so that should wrap up our list."

I studied it a moment, then added one last question mark. Markum said, "Who's that for?"

"There could be somebody involved in this that we don't know about, someone with a grudge against Gretel from another time and place in her life."

Markum took the pen from me and scratched through it.

"Why'd you do that?" I asked.

"Harrison, if somebody killed her we don't even know about, there's not a prayer in the world we'll find him, so it's not all that productive to spend time worrying about it, is it?"

I had to agree with his logic. I looked at the list again and studied the names: Runion, Hans, Graybill and Jorgenson. "So as far as we're concerned, it's one of these four."

"Like I said, I've got my money on Runion," Markum said.

"And I think Hans did it," I said. "It would help if I knew exactly where he was." I shook my head. "I just don't know what good it's going to do us. I've been digging into everyone's life who's been connected to Gretel since the newspaper accused me of killing her. What else can we do?"

Markum said, "I'll tell you exactly what I'm going to do. I'm going to go have a talk with Runion myself. I've got a feeling I might be able to get more out of him than you did, no offense."

"None taken," I said. "You're more than welcome to try."

"So what are you going to do?"

"I'm going to see if there's any way I can find out more about that clown. That's the real key to uncovering who killed Gretel."

Markum grinned at me. "How much do you want to bet it was Runion behind the greasepaint?"

"Let's see, I've got about ten bucks in my wallet. How's that sound?"

"Harrison, that's what I like about you. You're not afraid of high stakes."

"I just don't want to take any more of your money than I have to."

Markum said, "Let's touch base again later. I want to see if I can catch this developer before he takes off for the day."

"Be careful," I said.

"I didn't think you believed he did it."

I shrugged and asked, "What if I'm wrong? I don't want anything to happen to you because of me."

"Don't worry, I'll be on my toes. I promise you that."

After Markum was gone, I decided to call in a favor to see if I could find the identity of that lethal clown.

"Mary Fran, this is Harrison Black over at the candle-shop," I said after looking up the number for the local television station in the Micah's Ridge telephone book.

"Is my order in yet?" she asked. Mary Fran Duffy had just discovered the joys of pouring, and she was having a blast with the process. She was also a writer for our local news outlet, a cable team that was too small to support a channel of their own.

"No, the Christmas tree mold's been back-ordered again. Soon, I promise."

"So why are you calling?"

"I hate to ask, but I need a favor. I saw one of your cameramen shooting footage at the Founder's Day Celebration. Is there any chance I could come by and watch what they shot?"

Mary Fran didn't reply immediately, and I quickly added, "If there's a problem or if it's going to get you in any trouble, let's forget about it, okay?"

She said, "It's not that. The sheriff asked for the same thing last week. He watched our footage for an hour but he didn't find a thing on it. I'm afraid you'd be wasting your time."

"You could be right, but maybe we aren't looking for the same thing. Can I come by this evening?"

"Tell you what, it would be better if you could drop by in the morning. We're just about ready to shut down for the night. How early can you make it here?"

"I can be there at six," I said.

She groaned. "A.M.? You've got to be kidding. Come at seven, and bring two coffees with you."

"Should I bring anything for myself?" I asked.

"One of the coffees is for you, Harrison. See you tomorrow. Argh, at seven."

"Thanks, Mary Fran."

Maybe I'd be able to spot the clown in the video they'd shot, or maybe it would be a total waste of my time, but at the moment, it was the best thing I could come up with.

I WAS GLAD to see Eve when she came in later in the day to relieve me. I grabbed my coat and she said, "You're in an awful hurry. Do you have a big date tonight?"

I raised an eyebrow and said, "You're kidding, right? I haven't had a real date since I took over this place."

"Well then, what's the hurry?"

"Jubal Grant is shutting Flickering Lights down," I explained. "He's offered to sell me their stock at rock-bottom prices, but I've got to jump on it fast."

"Harrison, I should go with you. I know you've picked up a great deal working here, but I'm better versed in what things cost."

"Come on, Eve, don't you think I know that? I'll take a rough inventory, then we can come up with a price tomorrow morning." I suddenly remembered my appointment with Mary Fran at the television station. "I've got an errand to run first thing, but it shouldn't take too long. I promised Jubal we'd have a price for him by noon."

"What's the rush?" she asked as she hung her jacket up.

"He wants to be done with it, and he's only got forty-eight hours to clear out. I already told him he'd do better by having a big sale, but he's not interested. Jubal told me he just wants to get out of Micah's Ridge as quickly as he can."

Eve frowned, then after a few moments' thought, she said, "Here's what we'll do. After you take the inventory tonight, come back here and put the list on your desk. I'll come in early tomorrow and give you a figure we can live with before we open."

"I don't want to steal from him," I said. "This is going to be the only inheritance that Jubal gets."

Eve said, "As you've told me so many times before, we're not running a charity here, Harrison. But don't worry, I'll work up a fair price. Remember, though, he's the one who's demanding a quick sale. I'm taking that in to account, or you can figure it and come up with an offer yourself."

I'd been dreading the process of coming up with prices for a jumble of supplies. "No, I trust you'll be fair to him without bankrupting us. So, it looks like we're in the clear, doesn't it?"

"What, just because there isn't any competition left in town? Hickory's not that far away, Harrison, and you know all of the craft shops they have, not to mention what all's available in Charlotte. This is certainly no time to rest on our laurels."

"But it's still good news," I insisted.

"Yes, it's going to help us, there's no doubt about that."

I smiled. "That's all I wanted to hear. I'd better get over there. I've got a long night ahead of me as it is."

She said, "Hold on a second, I've got something that might help."

She disappeared into the office for a few minutes, then came out with six printed sheets. I took them and asked, "What's this?"

"It's something I've been working on for the shop. I've just about got it ready, but it needs a little tweaking before I'm ready to use it here."

The sheets had listed in neat entries everything we

stocked at the candleshop, from additives to wicks. "Wow, this is incredible."

She fought her smile, but I saw it creep in before she vanquished it. "I just thought it would make our lives easier when we ordered supplies."

"This is excellent. You've just saved me four or five hours of work."

"At least that," she said. "One thing, though. You should make a copy of this before you use it. It's my master list."

"You did this on a typewriter?" I asked.

"I'm not a big fan of computers," she said. "Just be careful with it."

I went back to the office and found a large envelope, then slid the sheets inside. "Thanks, this will help a lot."

"Go on, you've still got a lot of work to do."

I left the candleshop, happy for the first time in weeks. It actually felt like we were going to make a go of it. It was too bad that Gretel wouldn't have the chance to run her shop, and I honestly felt terrible about her death. But for now, I was feeling like At Wick's End was a going concern again.

Eighteen

"**H**AVE you ordered anything since you've been open?"
I asked Jubal as I studied his shelves.

"Gretel handled all that, I'm afraid. Is it worth your
while to make an offer?"

"I'll know better after I do a complete inventory list. It
shouldn't take too long."

He saw the sheets in my hand. "What are those?"

I handed the copies to him and said, "Eve made these
up for our shop."

"What a grand idea." He handed them back to me and
said, "Do you need my help?"

"No, I should be fine. You're not going anywhere, are
you?"

"I'll be right here. I've got scads of paperwork to complete for Hans."

"He's at least paying you for your work, isn't he?" I
wasn't sure how much of a legacy I'd be able to offer for
the meager supplies at the candleshop.

"Oh yes, I'm on the clock. I don't really need the money, but he's being such a nit about it all, I'm going to stick him for every hour I can. I daresay after this, we'll never see each other again."

I jumped all over that. "Then he's in town after all?"

Jubal looked startled by the notion. "Goodness no, he's still in South America. I suppose I should have said we won't have any contact with each other again. Now if you'll excuse me, I need to wade through this paperwork the attorney has saddled me with."

I started working in the front of the store and made my way toward the back, marking down quantities of each item there. Without Eve's sheets, I'd have been there three days, despite the low inventory level. As I worked, I glanced over at Jubal and felt sorry for him. He was studying a sheaf of legal documents, and I noticed he was nervously rubbing the bridge of his nose with one finger. I wouldn't trade places with him for all the money in the world. He caught me studying him, so I shot him a quick smile and got back to my work.

By 10 P.M., I had the lion's share of the work wrapped up. All that was left was what was in his storeroom. "Jubal, do you have a second?"

He marked his place in the document he was studying and said, "Certainly, Harrison, what can I do for you?"

"I just have the storeroom to do, but I was wondering if you might have a Coke or something around."

He said, "My goodness, here you're working late doing me a favor and I've completely ignored my duties as a host. Let me run down to the convenience store and get you something to drink. Are you hungry, too? I could order takeout and bring it back here."

My stomach rumbled, but I said, "No, I'm fine. Something to drink would be great."

"Nonsense, I insist. Do you know anything about this place called Slice of Heaven? I confess I've been meaning to try it, but I never seem to have the time. I'm starving myself."

I finally admitted, "A pizza would be great. I'll go pick it up, though."

"No, you keep working. You call it in and I'll go pick it up."

I grabbed his telephone and dialed April May's number. One of her waitresses answered, and I placed my order.

After I hung up the telephone, I said, "It'll be ready in twenty minutes."

"My, that's fast service."

"The owner prides herself on it. Be sure to tell them it's for me, I want credit for the order."

"I'm paying cash, Harrison. There's no need to use your credit account with them."

I smiled. "No, that's not it. I appreciate you buying, but the owner has a policy that for every ten pizzas you order, you get to request an old song for the jukebox."

"I'd heard about that, but I thought it was some kind of joke. What's this proprietress named?"

"April May, if you can believe it. You need to meet her before you leave Micah's Ridge. She's worth the trip herself."

"I'll be sure to ask for her by name," Jubal said. "Lock up after me, if you will. I'd hate to have a customer barge in on you while you're working."

"That's a good idea. Thanks for doing this."

"No sir, you're the one who deserves my thanks. You've helped a great deal. By this time tomorrow, Micah's Ridge will be a fading memory. No offense," he added hastily.

"None taken," I said. "I'm sure this hasn't been easy on you."

"Let's just say it will be a chapter I'm ready to close and leave it at that, shall we?"

After he was gone, I went back to my inventory, but my neck was stiff from bending over and peering at the shelves. I decided to walk around and stretch until Jubal came back with our late dinner. Maybe after I ate, I'd be in a better position to finish up and go home. As I walked around the shop, I wondered if Markum had managed to get more out of Runion than I had. I didn't want to admit it, but the big man could be persuasive when he put his mind to it. I still thought he was going after the wrong man, but I could be mistaken. If Hans were somewhere in town, surely he'd show up at the candleshop before Jubal left for good. How could he stay away? I glanced at the papers Jubal had been reading and saw that he'd been going over sale documents for the building. So Hans had him doing the preliminary work for selling the candleshop. The man had no end of nerve, and I didn't blame Jubal a bit for wanting to get out of there.

There was a tap on the door that startled me, and I saw Jubal outside, a pizza box in one hand and a six-pack of Cokes in the other. I let him in and he put it all down on the sales counter. "Thank you, Harrison. It was too awkward fishing for my keys. Did you finish yet?" he asked, glancing down at the papers he'd left.

"No, I just thought I'd take a break." I pointed to the papers and said, "I didn't mean to be nosy. I was just stretching. I can't believe Hans has the gall to have you handle the sale of the building, too."

Jubal laughed. "He wanted me to do more than that. He actually expected me to stay here for the next month until everything was wrapped up. I told him he didn't have enough money in his bank account to convince me to do that."

I grinned. "Good for you." I took a slice of pizza and put it on one of the plates. "So, what are your plans now?"

"Well, as I told you when I first moved here, I was just getting set to enjoy my retirement when Gretel called. I believe I'm going to revert to my previous plan and start traveling."

I took one of the Cokes and took a healthy swallow, then said, "Any place in particular you have in mind?"

"I've always wanted to visit the Florida Keys. There's a place called Big Pine Key that has the smallest deer in the world. There's just something about that idea that appeals to me."

I nodded and said, "I've heard all about the key deer. One of my customers, an artist named Ruby Hall, used to live down there. She adored them."

He ate a bite, then said, "It's the first of many travels I have in mind."

I took another bite, then asked, "Did you meet April when you picked up the pizza?"

"I did. If anything, you undersold her. She's quite an impressive woman, isn't she?"

I laughed. "That's a good word to describe her. What did she say when you told her I wanted credit for the pizza?"

"At first she refused, but then I saw she was just kidding. She also asked me to remind you about your selection. So it really is true, isn't it?"

"Scout's honor," I said, finishing off another piece of pizza. "That was great, but I'd better get back to work if we're going to get out of here by midnight."

Jubal pushed his own plate away. "I'm full, too. That was wonderful, though."

"It's good the next day for breakfast too," I said.

"By all means, take it home with you, then."

"I might just take you up on that," I said as I retrieved my list and got back to work. I was getting a second wind, so I finished up in less than an hour.

Jubal was dozing in his chair, and I coughed twice to wake him up. He looked disoriented for a second, then said, "I must have drifted off. Sorry I haven't been much help."

"Hey, you got the pizza, remember?" I tapped my list and added, "It's not going to be as much as I'd hoped. I can tell you that right now."

If he was disappointed, he hid it well. "To be honest with you, Harrison, I'd give it to you if it meant getting me out of here any sooner. Whatever you pay me will be my mad money for the first part of my trip. I'm in excellent financial shape, so don't worry about paying too much."

"Man, I've heard of reverse salesmanship, but you take it to a new level."

He smiled. "It's not that. I'm just happy Hans won't get his hands on this. I would ask one favor, though."

"Anything," I said as I gathered up my sheets.

"I'd like cash, if you don't mind. I never got around to opening an account around here, and I'll convert whatever you give me into traveler's checks at the first opportunity."

"I can do that. I'll swing by the bank before I come here." I wasn't sure about the exact total, but even if I gave him what the supplies cost, I knew I had enough in my personal account. It wasn't that I was all that well off, but I'd managed to save a little since taking over River's Edge, and I'd be able to pay myself back as we needed the supplies for the candleshop.

I looked at the pizza box and said, "Are you sure you don't want this?"

"Be my guest. I'd just have to throw out what's left if you didn't take it."

I picked it up and said, "We don't want that to happen, do we? I'll see you tomorrow, Jubal."

"Before noon, if you can make it."

"I'll do my best. I can't imagine it being a problem, but if an emergency comes up, I'll call you. We should be able to load everything here into the back of the truck."

We left the shop together, and I wished him a pleasant evening. He'd picked up regular Cokes, and I was used to the caffeine-free variety. I'd had two as I'd worked, and I was so wired up I doubted I'd be getting to sleep anytime soon. I thought about driving around some before going back to my apartment, and I soon found myself driving to Becka Lane's place. I'd heard she was out of the hospital, and knowing Becka, she'd be stubbornly ensconced in her apartment instead of heading for the safety of her sister's place. I knew if her hours were anything like they used to be, she'd still be up. Though I didn't want her to get the wrong idea, I did feel I should check up on her.

I could see as drove up that there was a light on in her apartment. I knocked twice, and was about ready to give up when she opened the door. Becka was usually dressed stylishly in the latest fashions, but tonight she wore an old sweatshirt and faded jeans. She'd never looked prettier, in my opinion, but I knew better than to tell her that.

"Harrison, what a pleasant surprise. What brings you out here?"

"I was in the neighborhood, so I thought I'd take a chance and show up unannounced. I thought you were going to your sister's place."

"I'm not letting anybody scare me away from my own apartment." She added, "I'm a mess, but you're welcome to come in if you'd like." Becka tried to smooth out her hair, but it was hard with one hand in a cast.

I stepped inside and she bolted the door behind me.

"Are you comfortable being here by yourself?" I asked.

"I'm fine, but I still have the feeling somebody's watching me. It's really eerie, you know?"

"I can't imagine. How are you feeling otherwise?"

"I've been better, but there's hope in sight." She winced as she moved to the couch.

"Did they give you anything for the pain?"

She nodded and pointed to a pair of pill bottles on the counter. "They did, but I'm trying to wait for bedtime before I take them. I've always been deathly afraid of pills."

How well I knew that. When we'd been dating, I could remember Becka not even liking to take aspirin, so I knew if she was taking something for the pain, it had to be more intense than she was letting on. "Why don't you take one now, and I'll stay until you get drowsy," I said.

"Would you? That would be so sweet."

She retrieved one pill, swallowed some water to chase it, then said, "They recommend two pills at a time, but I'm getting by on one." She came back to the couch and said, "It's been a crazy week, hasn't it? How's your life been?"

"You mean besides being accused of murder in the newspaper? I've had a dandy time," I said with a smile.

"You're too funny, Harrison." Before long she began to yawn. "I'm getting sleepy," she said. "Those pills are pretty strong. I can't imagine taking two."

"Can you stay awake long enough to deadbolt your door after I'm gone?"

"I will. I promise," she said.

I had a sudden impulse. "Becka, would you like me to stay here tonight? I could sleep on the couch."

"Don't be silly, I'm fine. Now go before I get too groggy to lock the door."

I started for the door, and she leaned forward to give me a gentle peck on the cheek. "Thanks for stopping by," she said.

I went back to my truck and headed home. I was halfway there when I realized my wallet wasn't where it should have been. It must have fallen out of my pocket. I pulled the truck over at a used car lot and used their parking lot lights to search the floor of the cab. No luck. I'd either left it at Becka's place or Jubal's shop, and since I didn't know where Jubal lived, I headed back to Becka's. I only hoped she hadn't fallen completely under the drug's spell.

Someone had taken my spot in front of her building, so I parked in the visitors' area and walked back toward Becka's. I was nearly at her unit when I saw something moving in the bushes in front of her place.

Was it an errant reflection of discarded trash, or was there something more ominous about its presence? I knew I was probably being paranoid, but after what Becka had been through, I didn't want to take any chances. For a moment I considered circling around the bushes and coming at the stranger from behind, but I quickly vetoed that notion. I stopped before I could be spotted and thought about what I should do. Then I realized I should find a telephone and call Morton. Let him take care of it. After all, it was his job, not mine.

I'd hoped to use Vince's phone to call, but either he wasn't home or, more likely, he was in too deep a sleep to hear my summons. One of these days I was going to have to break down and get a cell phone. I ran over to a nearby all-night laundermat and got the sheriff at his desk.

"Working around the clock now?" I asked, surprised to get the man himself.

"I'm just finishing up some paperwork and heading home. What's up?" He sounded like he was dead on his feet, and I hated adding to his troubles.

As calmly as I could, I said, "I think I found the man who's been stalking Becka Lane."

"Where are you?" he asked, the weariness suddenly gone from his voice.

"I'm close to her apartment. How soon can you get somebody over here?"

"I'm on my way home. I can get there before anyone else can. Harrison, let me handle this. Don't try to be a hero and do something stupid."

"Hey, that's why I called you. Hurry though, would you? I don't want him to get away."

"I'll be there in four minutes."

We were finally going to do something about this. "Good, I'll meet you out in front of the complex."

"Go home, Harrison. There's nothing else you can do."

"Either I go with you, or I'm going after this guy right now by myself."

He paused, then said, "You're a real pain in my rear, you know that? Okay, you can come, as long as you promise to stay out of my way."

Morton showed up three minutes later. He must have been flying.

"So where's this stalker?" he asked, carrying a long thick flashlight as he got out of the patrol car.

"He's in the bushes over by her place. Come on, follow me."

"Fine," he said, "but when we get close, you have to promise to stay back and let me handle it. Is that a deal?"

"I'm just here to watch."

We moved through the bushes as quietly as we could, but I still made more noise than Morton liked. There was enough light around us so that we could see where we were going, but the details of the landscape were all washed in dark gray. I found myself silently praying as we walked that the stalker hadn't gotten spooked for some reason and left. All I needed was Morton on my back about creating false alarms.

I thought we'd overshot the stalker hidden in the bushes, or worse yet, lost him altogether, when Morton suddenly stopped dead in his tracks. I started to say something when he shook his head quickly. Pointing ahead to the shadows, I saw what I had missed on first glance.

Becka's stalker was still there, hovering in the bushes, patiently watching for her.

Nineteen

MORTON turned on his flashlight and illuminated the suspect's back. "I'm Sheriff Morton. Put your hands up and turn around. Slowly."

I saw that the man standing there had something in his hand that looked like a crowbar. He started to tense as if to turn and fight or run, and Morton wasn't going to allow either action.

"I said drop it! I've got a gun at your back. You don't stand a chance."

The crowbar dropped to the ground and the man turned slowly around to face us.

It was Vince, Becka's maintenance man. He said, "I'm glad you got here. I've been watching Becka's place, but somebody needs to relieve me."

"Come on, you actually think we're going to believe you're here to help?" Morton said.

"He *has* been protective of her," I said. "I can't imagine him threatening her."

Morton wasn't buying it, though. "Then why is he hiding in the bushes? Come on, you're coming with me."

Vince's face got red in the light. "Get that thing out of my eyes. I told you, I'm here to watch out for her."

"Then you've got nothing to worry about, do you?"

Vince said angrily, "You're not going to cuff me. I'd rather get shot."

Morton said icily, "It's your call."

I saw his hand tense on the handle and I said, "Vince, you'd better do what he says."

"Yeah, Vince, listen to your buddy here."

All of the fight seemed to go out of him as Morton put the cuffs on him. As we walked back to the police car, he kept protesting his innocence, but Morton acted like he couldn't hear a word.

I said, "What should I do?"

"Go home, Harrison. We caught the bad guy."

Vince didn't respond to the bait. I said, "But what if you're wrong?"

Morton replied, "Then she's no worse off than she was before."

I watched them drive away, then I remembered my wallet. That was just what I needed, getting a ticket for driving without a license after what had just happened. I took a chance and walked back to Becka's, not really expecting her to answer, but not really having much choice, either.

To my surprise, she opened the door before I could even knock. "What was that all about?" she asked as I stepped inside.

"I thought you'd be asleep," I said.

"I should have taken two pills after all. As soon as you left, I was wide awake again. I heard voices out here, but I wasn't about to come out. Was that Vince the cop arrested?"

"He was hiding in the bushes watching your place," I said. "He claims he was just trying to protect you, but the sheriff doesn't believe it."

Becka shivered. "Is your offer to stay over still open? I don't think I'd be able to sleep a wink after this."

"I'd be happy to stay till morning," I said. "All I need is a blanket and a pillow and I'll be fine."

"Thank you, Harrison. For everything."

I nodded, and she quickly got me settled on the couch. After we said our good nights, I lay there wondering if Vince was a protector or a stalker. If I'd gone after him by myself, I knew I would have believed his story. He was that convincing.

I'd drifted off, and Becka's telephone brought me abruptly awake. "Hello?"

"Harrison, is that you?" It was Sheriff Morton. "What did you do, decide to move in and make yourself at home?"

"Becka was afraid to stay by herself, so I'm bunking on the couch."

Morton said, "She had every right to be concerned. This guy's definitely the one who's been stalking her."

"He confessed?" I asked, still shocked that I'd misread the super.

"Not at first, but after we ran his prints through the computer, he caved soon enough. It turns out Vince is really Vance Gregory, a man with two outstanding warrants in California. Care to guess what they were for?"

"Stalking," I said.

"Hey, you got it right on the first try."

I took a deep breath, then said, "You were right. I was wrong."

"About Vince? Don't sweat it, the guy's a born con-man. You found him hiding in the bushes, and that brought him to our attention. You did a good thing tonight, Harrison."

Compliments were rare enough from the sheriff, but I wasn't in the mood to accept any. I'd completely mis-judged the man. In fact, the only thing I had done right was calling the sheriff into it.

Still, Becka's troubles were over. That was what counted. I thought about waking her up and sharing what I'd learned, but I finally decided to let her get a good night's sleep before breaking the news to her. It was the only way I'd manage to get any more sleep that night myself, now that it looked like the threat was finally over.

BECKA CAME OUT the next morning and woke me up. "Hey, don't you have a candleshop to run?"

I glanced at the clock and saw that even if I were at my apartment, I wouldn't make it to the studio for my ap-pointment in time. I said, "Give me a second to get dressed, would you?"

"You never struck me as the shy type before," she said.

"Well, I am now."

She shrugged, then walked back into her bedroom while I hastily pulled on my pants. I was just buttoning my shirt when she walked back in again. "Are you decent yet?"

"Come on out. There's something we need to talk about before I go."

"Harrison, I'm sorry, I shouldn't have been teasing you. I just can't remember sleeping that soundly."

"You might want to sit down. I've got something shocking to tell you."

She did as she was told, perching on the edge of the loveseat that matched the sofa I'd slept on. "What is it?"

"The sheriff and I found your stalker last night. He's sitting in jail right now."

A wave of emotions crossed her face. "You're serious, aren't you? How can that be? Who was it?"

"I told you we found the super hiding in the bushes last night. Well, it turns out Vince is wanted in California for stalking two other women. When the sheriff confronted him, he confessed to it all, including pushing you off the jogging path. He wasn't all that pleased about you coming to me and not him."

Becka sat there, as if she was in shock. "I don't understand. How did you know to come back?"

"I thought I'd left my wallet here," I confessed. "When I came back to get it, I saw someone in the bushes watching you, but he didn't see me. I called Morton and we got him." I was feeling a little guilty about taking all of the credit. "The guy was smooth. I was ready to believe he was just looking out for you, but the sheriff saw right through him."

"You called Morton, though, didn't you? Thank you, Harrison."

She stood and kissed me solemnly. I broke it off before it could develop into anything else. I wasn't going there again with her. "You're most welcome. Listen, I hate to run out on you, but I'm really running late."

"Go. I'll be fine now."

If I hurried, I'd just be fifteen minutes late for my appointment with Mary Fran at the television station. I couldn't do anything about my wrinkled clothes, but I did manage to get my hair tamed before I went in. My wallet hadn't turned up at Becka's. I just hoped it was at Flickering Lights.

"There you are," Mary Fran said as hurried in. "I was about to give up on you."

"Sorry I'm late. I overslept."

"No harm done," she said. "I've got the tape set up in our editing room."

She led me back through a hallway full of old equipment, then ducked into a room not much bigger than a telephone booth.

After explaining how to run the machinery, she said, "If you want a hard copy of something you see, just hit the print button and it comes out here. I've got to charge you a dollar a copy, so make sure it's a shot you want. Good luck. Or should I say happy hunting?"

"I'll take either one at this point," I said.

The start of the tape showed the interview with the mayor of New Conover. I'd seen him around the fair, but he didn't interest me a bit. I was more intent on watching what was going on behind the scenes. I fast-forwarded through the interview, caught a few candid conversations with vendors and visitors, and then I saw the camera sweep across the area just behind Gretel as the cameraman caught an image of the murder scene. Something was different about the picture, but it took me a second to realize what it was. I had something, but I wasn't sure if it would be enough. I hit the print button so I'd have a copy to check later, then continued scanning the tape.

In another few moments, I was confronted with the static of a dead tape.

There were only nine minutes on the tape, and I hadn't seen the hint of a clown anywhere, though I had found something worth exploring. I watched the tape twice more and was ready to give up finding the assassin on tape when something caught my eye in the background. Yes, there was no doubt about it. In one corner of the picture was the clown Evelyn had described to me, the same man I'd nearly fallen over at the fair. I hurried back to Mary Fran and said, "I think I might have something, but it's tough to see. Is there any way to enhance this?"

She nodded, "There is, but I can't do it. Let's get Tom." We found an older engineer in the backroom repairing a computer motherboard. Mary Fran said, "Tom, do you have a second?"

"I'm tied up right now. Sorry."

I started to say something when Mary Fran shushed me. To her coworker, she said, "It's okay. I shouldn't have bothered you." Then she turned to me and said, "He couldn't have enhanced it, anyway. The tape's too grainy. Sorry, Harrison."

Tom put his soldering iron back in its stand and said, "What are you talking about?"

She said, "You're busy, it's nothing you need to worry about."

Tom replied, "If there's something on a tape you want to see, I can bring it up for you. Let's go have a look."

Mary Fran was smiling as Tom walked by, and I thanked her silently. There wasn't room for all three of us in the tape editing room, so Mary Fran stood outside in the hallway. Tom cued up the tape and said, "What are you looking for?"

I pointed toward the screen and he slapped at my finger. "Don't touch that. Just tell me."

"Do you see the clown in one corner? I need a better look at him."

Tom said, "You pulled me away from my work so we could look at clowns? You've got to be kidding." He fiddled with some dials as he complained, and the clown jumped into intense clarity. He did something else to move the entire tape over to one side, and I could now see all of the clown in the display.

"Can you run the tape this way?"

He didn't say anything, but tapped another button and I saw the clown moving in reverse. When the start of the shot arrived and the scene shifted, he started it again.

"There's no audio here, just background noise," he said.

"I'm not expecting him to say anything," I said. I watched as the clown sat down on the courthouse steps, much as I'd found him the day Gretel had been shot.

And then I saw something that told me, without a doubt, who had killed Gretel Barnett.

I forgot myself and pointed to the screen again. "Freeze it right there. I need a copy of that."

Tom froze it, hit the copy button and handed me the print. I wasn't sure it was evidence that would hold up in any court of law, but I was convinced.

"Thanks, you two, you've helped more than you'll ever know."

They both looked bewildered by my behavior as I handed Mary Fran two dollars, but there was no time to explain. I had a murderer to confront.

I tried to get the sheriff, but he wouldn't come to the telephone. Evidently Vince or Vance or whatever his real name was confessing to crimes that no one had the slightest idea he'd ever committed. I considered getting one of Morton's deputies to back me up, but I really didn't know any of them well enough to share my theory with.

I made up my mind to confront the man myself. After all, it was broad daylight in a busy part of town. He wouldn't have the nerve to try anything with the world walking past his front door.

Twenty

"HARRISON, I trust you've brought the cash with you," Jubal said as I walked into his store.

"I've got it right here," I said, patting my back pocket. "I'm just sorry it couldn't be more."

"My friend, I already told you, whatever you came up with will be fine with me."

I kept my back to the glass, making sure I was always in sight of the street, as I said casually, "Of course, you've got the rest of your inheritance to see you through, don't you?"

He looked at me oddly. "I thought we'd already discussed this. Gretel didn't leave me a thing."

"As Jubal, no, but as Hans, you're going to make a real killing when you sell this building to Runion, not to mention getting everything else Gretel had."

Jubal said, "Harrison, I'm afraid you've been out in the sun too long. I'm not Hans."

"Come on, there's nobody here but the two of us. Do you honestly think you're going to get away with this?"

He eased up to the register as he said, "I truly don't know what you're talking about."

"Okay, if you want me to lay it out for you, I will. You see, I knew you killed Gretel before I realized who you were. It wasn't until after I figured out you were the murderer that I realized that meant you had to be Hans."

He kept fidgeting with something, but I was on a roll. I pulled out the photograph, laid it on the counter and said, "You were the clown I saw that day at the fair. One of your customers came by here to buy some supplies, but you were closed, though you denied it later to me. I told you, candlemakers can be a persistent lot. When she saw you were gone, she went to the fair to buy her supplies there. She was talking to Gretel just before you killed her."

He looked at the copy and said, "How could you possibly think I'm the person behind this clown makeup, let alone prove it?"

I pointed to the photograph and said, "You mean besides the fact that you used to work on a carnival? I'm sure you learned how to apply that makeup; you did a first-class job when I saw you."

"And what makes you think that?"

"In a way, Gretel provided that clue herself. She made a diary entry on her web page with your bio on it. I'd forgotten all about it until this morning. It fits, but there's more to it than that. You're rubbing the bridge of your nose in this photograph, just like you did last night. I figure it's a nervous habit. You probably don't even realize you're doing it."

His hand started to go to his nose, but stopped halfway there. "And you call this proof? The police are convinced

Pearly killed Gretel. It could just have easily been him in the clown makeup."

"Come on, I found the tube you planted under his workbench. Micah's Ridge isn't that big. I'm willing to bet there's a pretty good chance one of the clerks at Party World will be able to identify you. It's not going to come to that, though, is it? Your fingerprints are going to give you away as Hans Barnett, not Jubal Grant. That's why you wanted cash today, wasn't it? It's the same reason Jubal Grant didn't get anything in Gretel's will; he doesn't exist."

"So what," the man said. "That still doesn't prove I killed her. Where's the gun?"

"You were pretty clever about that, I'll give you credit there. I've got a feeling I know where you stashed it, though."

"You're bluffing," Hans said fiercely.

"Don't you wish. You see, I noticed something else when I was looking at the video taken on the day of the fair. That cannon had a plug in its barrel that wasn't there when I set up that morning. You made something to fit, shoved the gun in during the confusion and capped it with your homemade plug just in case you were stopped. It was pretty clever of you. Did you plan to retrieve it on your way out of town?"

Instead of replying, I finally saw what he was digging for by the register, and I couldn't believe how stupid I'd been. It was a boning knife, not much of a weapon against the police and their guns, but it was more than I had.

I tried to keep my voice calm as I said, "What are you going to do with that? If you kill me, the police will come looking for you."

The man smiled and said, "No, I believe they'll come

looking for Jubal, and the second I walk out that door, he's not going to exist anymore."

"You'll have to kill both of us," Pearly said as he came out of the backroom.

I don't know who was more surprised to see him, Hans or me. As the knife wavered in his hand, he said, "How did you get back there?"

"You really should lock your rear exit," he said.

"It was locked."

Pearly smiled and joined me at the front door. "But not deadbolted. I managed to force the lock with a screwdriver and come in."

"But how did you know?" I asked.

"I've been following you for the last two days. I knew if anyone figured this mess out, it would be you." He turned to Hans and said, "There's no way you're going to get both of us."

Hans considered doing just that, then he bolted for the back. I started after him but Pearly grabbed my arm. In a minute I knew why. We walked to the back of the shop and I saw Morton slapping the handcuffs on the murderer.

"You're here, too," I asked. "What happened to Vince?"

"I figured he was safe enough locked up in a cell. Pearly waved me down in the street a few minutes ago and I almost ran him over. If I hadn't heard it out of this guy's mouth himself, I still probably wouldn't have believed it."

"He wanted to arrest me, but I insisted he come with me first," Pearly said with a smile. "As soon as I heard what you two were discussing, I ducked out for assistance."

"Let's go," Morton said to Hans. "We'll go out the front way this time."

Hans said, "Surely you don't believe any of this."

"Let's just say I'm willing to pursue it long enough to find out who you really are."

Hans shook his head in disgust. He knew he was caught.

I had to add, "If you hadn't been greedy wanting to sell those supplies, I wouldn't have put it all together until it was too late. Think about that when you're rotting away in jail for murder."

He lunged at me then, but Morton had a good hold on the cuffs and jerked him back.

The sheriff looked at me and said, "Now, Harrison, what have I told you in the past? Don't poke the bear. Listen, hang around a minute until I can get a black-and-white over here."

After they were gone, Pearly said, "So what happens now? Did you actually buy this inventory from him?"

I shook my head. "No, I didn't figure it was his to sell since he came by it through murder."

"So what do we do now?" Pearly asked.

"We wait for the deputy, then we get you back to River's Edge. We've missed having you there, my friend."

"And I've missed being there," he said. He held my wallet up and said, "Did you miss this yet?"

I took it and said, "Where'd you find it?"

"It was in the backroom. I thought you might be needing it."

"Thanks," I said.

Sheriff Morton came back alone. "He's on his way to the station. Listen, I want to say something to both of you while I've got the chance."

"There's no need to apologize," I said.

Morton looked startled by the suggestion. "What makes you think I owe you an apology?"

Pearly said, "Let's see, you practically accused us both of murder. Isn't that a good place to start?"

Morton shook his head. "This is why I hate working

with amateurs. I was just doing my job. I don't make any excuses for that."

"So what did you want to say?"

"I wanted to thank you both for your help, but I'm not sure I still want to."

I grinned at him. "It's too late now, isn't it?"

Pearly asked, "So what's going to happen to all this?"

Morton shrugged. "It's not any of my business. Now let's get out of here. I've got an officer in back to watch the place until we can lock it up. Somebody did a real number on the lock in back. I wonder who that could have been."

Pearly said, "I wonder."

We left Morton, and Pearly and I drove our vehicles back to River's Edge. We met again on the front steps, and Pearly said, "Harrison, I don't know how I'll ever repay you."

"I'm not the only one here who believed in you. We all knew you were innocent."

"Based on what? I have to admit, the evidence did seem to point in my direction."

I slapped him on the back. "Yeah, but when your family's in trouble, you stand behind them. That's what we all did."

"Then I'm glad to be a member of this particular clan."

Eve must have spotted us outside. She came bustling over, glanced at Pearly and told him, "It's high time you stopped skulking around here."

Before Pearly could reply, Eve turned to me and said, "I stayed up most of the night, but I've got the pricing done. You just need to plug in the inventory numbers and we'll be set."

I didn't know how to tell her that the deal had fallen through, but she must have read something on my face. "Harrison Black, I can't believe you let this slip out of your hands. Just when we have the chance to make some headway, you manage yet again to snatch defeat from the jaws of victory."

She stormed back to the candleshop, and it was all Pearly and I could do to hold our laughter in until she was gone.

Pearly said, "Now I really feel like I'm back home."

Dorothea Hurley's Top-Secret
Apple Pan Dowdy Recipe

(The one that Millie borrowed)

1/3 cup brown sugar
1/4 teaspoon nutmeg
1/4 teaspoon cinnamon
3 cups sliced and peeled apples (tart works well, one or two
apples are plenty, depending on their size)
1/3 cup sugar
3/4 cup flour
3/4 teaspoon baking powder
1/4 teaspoon salt
1/4 cup shortening (we use real butter)
1 egg
1/3 cup milk

Combine the brown sugar, nutmeg and cinnamon. Coat the sliced apples in the brown sugar–nutmeg–cinnamon mix. Preheat oven, then place apple mixture in a buttered 1-quart baking dish and bake covered for 30 minutes at 375 degrees.

In a separate bowl, mix the sugar, flour, baking powder and salt. Cut in the softened shortening (butter), and add the egg and milk. Stir until well mixed, then spread over the apples (still in their dish) and bake uncovered for another 30 minutes, still at 375 degrees.

This was one of my late mother-in-law's desserts, still a real family favorite at our house. Some folks like to pour a little cold milk over their portion, but I like a glass of milk on the side.

Assorted Candlemaking Tips
for Gel Candles

By adjusting the temperature of the wax, you can get some interesting shapes and forms in the candle using the wax itself.

Play with different temperatures to get a varying amount of bubbles in the wax. For undersea candles, a popular choice for gel wax, we pour the wax as soon as it's melted. That gives lots and lots of bubbles.

Sometimes we make small amounts of vivid wax combinations; pour the heated wax on a cookie sheet and let the different colors cool. The wax stays thin, around one-eighth inch. Then we cut out shapes from the wax and stick them to the insides of the glass. It provides a bright kaleidoscope of colors when clear gel wax is poured into the candle.

Themed candles are fun for holidays, birthdays and any special occasion. Craft stores have a variety of small objects that do well added to a gel wax pour. We've done themes with semiprecious stones, marbles, pretty gravel, colored sand and other items we already had on hand.

An assortment of coins buried into the gel wax make a good theme. Costume jewelry and anything that can stand the heat of the pour are good choices as well.

Handcrafted
Candle Stands and Bases

Sometimes the way a candle is displayed is more important than the candle itself. Just about anything that will hold a candle upright can be crafted into a base. In the past, I've made candleholders out of papier-mâché, flower pots and even punched tin. I've found that recycled jars and bottles also make perfect candleholders.

Using a little creativity, you can customize your base to the occasion. For Halloween, decorate jars with ghosts, goblins and full moons after painting the glass black. To make a specialized holder for Christmas, a red or green base frosted with flocking makes a perfect centerpiece. Remember, though, that anything you put close to the candle's wick needs to be fireproof!

I've also seen fruit carved out to hold candles at parties. The only limit is your own imagination, so have fun and experiment.

Look for the next
Candlemaking Mystery

A Flicker of Doubt

by Tim Myers, coming in June 2006

One

WHEN my kayak brushed against the woman's body, I thought I'd hit another half-submerged log. The Gunpowder River was full of all kinds of debris, washed there from the banks in the heavy rains that had assaulted us over the past two weeks. It wasn't until I looked closer that I realized what it really was.

In a moment of panic I dropped my paddle, but caught it again before it skittered off the sleek surface of the boat and into the water. Without it, I'd be hopelessly adrift.

"Harrison, what's wrong?"

I looked over to the shore and saw Markum standing near the concrete steps that led down to the water. He was one of my tenants in the River's Edge complex, a converted warehouse that featured retail businesses downstairs and offices upstairs; my apartment was on that floor, too. My great-aunt Belle had left me the entire place, along with the At Wick's End candleshop I ran, and a hefty mortgage on it all.

"Somebody's floating in the water," I shouted inanely. "She's dead. What should I do?"

Markum considered it for a moment, then said, "I could call the sheriff, but it's hard to tell how far the body will drift by the time he gets here. Do you have any rope with you?"

"Yes," I admitted reluctantly, understanding instantly what he had in mind. I was a candlemaker by trade. The worst things I had to deal with in my business were wax burns and nasty customers; nothing in my life had prepared me for what I was facing. Markum was a self-proclaimed expert in salvage and recovery, though I'd never been able to pin him down much more than that on what he did from day to day. He didn't sound at all panicked by the situation, but then again, he was standing safely on shore while I was the one drifting six inches from a dead body.

"You've got to bring her in," he said.

"I know that," I shouted a little more harshly than I'd meant to. I wasn't sure I was up to the task, but I didn't really have much choice. I reached behind me and retrieved the rope I kept on board to tie the kayak up while I went exploring some of the Gunpowder's coves. Once I had the rope in my hand, I wondered how I was going to tether her securely enough to pull her to shore.

Markum called out, "Harrison, I hate to bring this up, but you're drifting away at a pretty good clip. It's not going to get any easier."

I hated it when he was right. Judging from the general area where I'd found her, if I delayed too long, I might not be able to pull her weight through the water back upstream. Where could I attach the rope, though? Should I tie it to her hand? I shuddered at the thought. No way. How about her leg? No, that was too gruesome to even consider.

There was a belt on her dress; maybe it would hold until I got her to shore. I hastily tied my rope through it, then started paddling backward toward the steps of the complex.

I'd covered less than a dozen feet when my load suddenly got lighter. Blast it all, the belt had come off and I could see the woman drifting downstream again. I paddled back toward her, not daring to look at Markum. For some reason I was furious with him. Then I realized it was probably because he was standing there on land and I was wrestling with a body in the water.

I approached again, then noticed to my horror that when the belt had come loose, it had flipped her over in the water.

A stranger would have been bad enough, but I knew this woman, and knew her all too well.

AUTHOR BIOGRAPHY

Tim Myers lives with his family near the Blue Ridge Mountains he loves and writes about. He is the award-winning author of the Agatha-nominated Lighthouse Inn mystery series and the Candlemaking mystery series, as well as over seventy short stories.

Tim has been a stay-at-home dad for the last fourteen years, finding time for murder and mayhem whenever he can.

To learn more, visit his website at www.timmyers.net or contact him at timothylmyers@hotmail.com.

The Candlemaking Mystery
series by

Tim Myers

Each book includes candlemaking tips!

At Wick's End

0-425-19460-4

Harrison Black has to learn the art of
candlemaking fast when he inherits his Great-Aunt
Belle's shop, At Wick's End. But when someone
breaks into the apartment Belle left him, Harrison
begins to suspect that her death may not have
been an accident.

Snuffed Out

0-425-19980-0

When the power goes out in Harrison Black's
candle shop, he find his tenant electrocuted.
Now, as the tenant's death starts to look like
murder, Harrison will burn the candle at both
ends to catch a killer.

**Available wherever books are sold or at
penguin.com**